"*A sense of belonging,*"
she murmured.

"I want to marry you, Ashley. Will you think about that while you mix with your friends tonight?"

"Harry...." It was a breathless little gasp, as though he'd punched the air out of her lungs.

Her eyes widened wonderingly.

"Don't answer me now. I just want you to know," he said with quiet seriousness. To imprint it firmly on her mind, he repeated, "I want to marry you."

EMMA DARCY nearly became an actress, until her fiancé declared he preferred to attend the theater with her. She became a wife and mother. Later, she took up oil painting—unsuccessfully, she remarks. Then she tried architecture, designing the family home in New South Wales, Australia. Next came romance writing—"the hardest and most challenging of all the activities," she confesses.

Books by Emma Darcy

HARLEQUIN PRESENTS

1659—A WEDDING TO REMEMBER
1679—IN NEED OF A WIFE
1721—BURNING WITH PASSION
1745—THE FATHERHOOD AFFAIR
1771—CLIMAX OF PASSION
1785—LAST STOP MARRIAGE

EMMA DARCY

Mischief and Marriage

Harlequin Books

TORONTO • NEW YORK • LONDON
AMSTERDAM • PARIS • SYDNEY • HAMBURG
STOCKHOLM • ATHENS • TOKYO • MILAN
MADRID • WARSAW • BUDAPEST • AUCKLAND

Dedicated to my
beloved husband, Frank,
who shared all the
stories of great love with me.

ISBN 0-373-11815-5

MISCHIEF AND MARRIAGE

First North American Publication 1996.

Copyright © 1996 by Emma Darcy.

This edition published by arrangement with Harlequin Books S.A.

Printed in U.S.A.

Dear Reader,

Four years ago my husband became very ill with a rare condition that affected his whole system. It was a devastating blow, but we determined then to find all the joy we could in the time that was left to us. It was especially hard when my husband lost most of his vision, but he could still live the stories I read to him in his mind.

Through it all he wanted the stories to go on, to give what he could to them. *Mischief and Marriage* was our last book together and features a ghost. My husband made up the rules for ghostland. One of them was that love knew no boundaries. The only boundaries that existed were those that people imposed themselves.

My husband passed away on 14th March 1995.

I hope that reading *Mischief and Marriage* brings you as much joy as it brought to Frank and me while we were creating it.

Best wishes,

Emma Darcy

CHAPTER ONE

IT WAS a butler's duty, George Fotheringham assured himself, to remind the master of the house of *his* duty. It was a touchy subject, a highly touchy subject, but after this last near fatal incident, the matter had to be raised.

It wasn't that Master Harry was irresponsible. He had a good heart. If Miss Penelope hadn't succumbed to her tragic illness, everything would have been quite different. Nevertheless, the indisputable fact that Master Harry now took life far too lightly could not be ignored any longer. It was three years since Miss Penelope's sad demise. It was time for this frivolous recklessness to stop.

'May I point out, sir, you could have been killed in the avalanche,' George began with portentous emphasis. 'To risk skiing in uncertain conditions...well, it is improvident, sir. It may not be of any concern to you, sir, but there is the matter of an heir to be considered. I wondered if you might give it some thought.'

Harold Alistair Cliffton almost sighed. He remembered his cracked ribs in time and eyed his butler wearily instead. 'Sorry, George. I'm not up to getting married at the moment.'

Not up to anything, he thought, staring broodingly into the huge log fire that kept the chill of winter at bay. *The winter of my discontent.* Impossible to remove that chill deep within his soul.

Having been rendered immobile with a broken leg, not to mention the damaged rib cage and some internal bruising, boredom was fast setting in. And depression. It had been a bad choice to convalesce at Springfield Manor. It conjured up too many memories of Pen and their last months together when each day had been so precious. Now...he didn't care if he saw another day.

'I wouldn't presume to tell you what to do, sir. I merely propose that you consider possible outcomes,' George persisted, determined on raising Master Harry's awareness of what would result should he die prematurely.

There was no response.

George frowned. He had to focus Master Harry's attention on the future. It was a matter of position and positioning. The agreement between the Cliffton family and his own was extremely significant to George, and to his mind, Master Harry had a solemn duty to fulfil his part of it.

The connection between their two families dated back to the Battle of Flodden in 1513, when Henry Cliffton had joined the Earl of Surrey in fighting the invading army of James IV of Scotland. In a violent melee with the Scottish pikemen, it was George's brave ancestor, Edward Fotheringham, who had saved the life of Henry Cliffton, fighting off the fierce attackers from where the nobleman lay wounded. It was promised then and there, from that day onwards, Edward Fotheringham and his descendants could always find employment in the service of Henry Cliffton and his descendants.

In today's uncertain world with its shifting values, security was not to be scoffed at. George thought of his two sons, fine boys both of them, doing well at school. They had their expectations, and rightly so. He cleared his throat and pressed his case.

'We do need an heir so that the family traditions can be maintained. An heir, sir, is not so much an obligation, but a duty,' George stated with the gravity due to such an important issue.

The words must have penetrated. Master Harry looked up, cocking a quizzical eyebrow. 'What precisely are you suggesting, George? I doubt that any of my charming female acquaintances would care to have a child out of wedlock in order to ensure that your heirs and assigns have continuing employment for the next few generations.'

George took a deep breath, apprehensive about giving offence, yet deeply conscious of all that could be lost. For centuries, a distinguished line of butlers from his family had served the Cliffton family at Springfield Manor. For that long line of honourable service, and all its concomitant advantages, to be now looking at an uncertain future was unacceptable.

Besides, Master Harry needed an interest, a serious interest that would involve him in a very real sense of continuity again. Having children and bringing up an heir to take over from him would give him a purpose for living.

George played his master card. 'I have taken the liberty, sir, of investigating the Australian branch of your family.'

Harry looked startled, then threw his head back and laughed. 'How enterprising of you, George! Better a descendant of the Black Sheep than no heir at all.'

'Absolutely!' George fervently agreed, the burden of having taken such an initiative considerably lightened by Master Harry's amused response. 'It would, of course, be a preferable resolution were you to marry, sir, if only a marriage of convenience for the purpose of...'

'My sense of duty doesn't stretch that far,' Harry said dryly. 'Don't keep me in suspense. Tell me the fruits of your investigation. Were there any fruits?'

At least he had sparked some interest, George observed with satisfaction. Hope burgeoned in his heart. Master Harry must surely begin to appreciate what had to be done.

'As I recall the story,' Harry mused, 'our Black Sheep was a shameless rake. It was his scandalous affair with the Duchess of Buckingham that led to his being disinherited and exiled.'

'Quite right, sir.' To George's mind, the unworthiness of this branch of the family had to be glaringly evident. 'He was a cad and a bounder. He kissed and told. A disgrace to the escutcheon, sir.'

The point didn't seem to have the desired effect. Master Harry appeared enthused. 'There must be a veritable host of heirs we could call upon Down Under. A hundred years of going forth and multiplying should have produced...' He grinned. 'How many, George?'

'The 1917 influenza epidemic wiped most of them out, sir. One could say we are as much at the end of the line in Australia as we are in Britain. There is a boy, sir. A nine-year-old schoolboy. Such a young child is hardly a safeguard against the ultimate calamity. It will be many years before he can father a child himself, whereas you...'

'But consider, George!' There was a teasing twinkle in Harry's eyes, brightening their blue to a lively hue. 'He's young enough for you to train him up to your standards. You could mould yourself a splendid master who would be everything you wanted him to be.'

George sighed. He had hoped to stir some pride in Master Harry's direct blood line by using the Australian boy as a spur. There was no doubt in George's mind that Master Harry could have his pick of any number of suitable young ladies whom he had entertained at Springfield Manor in latter years.

'You are not dead yet, sir,' he stated flatly.

'We know not the hour nor the day, George,' Harry replied flippantly. 'Clearly the most provident course is to fetch the boy over here so he'll become acquainted with his inheritance.'

'It is not quite so straightforward as that, sir,' George demurred, deeply vexed at the turn his attempt at subtle pressure had taken. 'The boy has a widowed mother. His father, who was the last direct heir, drowned some years ago. The woman has her own home, runs a modestly successful business and is certainly attractive enough to have formed another attachment. Should she marry again... Well, it will be very messy getting the boy over here.'

'I'll bet you a bottle of 1860 Madeira that I can fetch them here, George.'

Such levity grated deeply on George's sense of propriety. The wine cellar at Springfield Manor was of particular pride to him. One of the finest, if not *the* finest, private cellars in England. Master Harry had to be joking about giving everything up to what had to be an unworthy strain of the family.

'It really would be much simpler, sir, were you to marry and have a decent number of children to ensure a succession of the family.'

Harry grinned. 'Did you get photographs of the boy and his mother, George?'

'There is no family likeness, sir. None at all.'

'The photographs, George.' Harry's curiosity was piqued. 'I want to see them.'

George had a very nasty premonition. He recognised the light of mischief in Master Harry's eyes. He had been witness to it on many an occasion. What followed was invariably mayhem of one kind or another. He had been a venturesome boy and he had become even more dangerously ven-

turesome once the benevolent influence of Miss
Penelope's lovely nature had passed away with her.

It had been a mistake to confess to the Australian
investigation. It had been a mistake to present
Master Harry with any kind of challenge. George
knew it was all his own fault when his premonition
proved right several hours later.

'Make inquiries about flights to Australia, will
you, George? It's summer over there, isn't it? I
rather fancy a bit of summer. As soon as I can get
this cast off my leg I'll be on my way.'

Master Harry's earlier gloom had completely
dissipated. He was in fine fettle. 'Might get in a
few days' cricket, as well. Make a note of the dates
for the test matches between England and
Australia, please, George. If there's one in Sydney,
I could take young William with me to watch the
game. A nine-year-old should take a lively interest
in cricket.' He grinned at George. 'Fine name,
William.'

Mischief! That was what he was up to. Mischief
instead of marriage. And where would it all end if
Master Harry's meddling caused mayhem?

CHAPTER TWO

ASHLEY Harcourt didn't know that today was to mark the beginning of a completely different phase in her life. Her desk calendar looked the same as usual. It bore no big red letters to give warning of something momentous about to happen. There was no sense of premonition hovering in her mind.

She *was* faced with a particularly nasty piece of work in the person of Gordon Payne, who was sitting in her home office, filling the chair on the other side of her desk and voicing a string of complaints. But she was ready to deal with that. More than ready.

Giving satisfaction was a high professional priority to Ashley. She prided herself on running her employment agency effectively, fitting the right people into the right jobs. But there was a limit, a very definite limit, to how much satisfaction any one person could demand from another.

Ashley had precisely formed opinions on this point. She was twenty-nine years old, had worked hard to build up her own business after being widowed and had dealt with a great many people in a wide variety of situations. Satisfaction in any relationship was a two-way street, a compatible, complementary give-and-take situation.

14

As she listened to Gordon Payne revealing himself in his true colours, she silently berated herself for a bad mistake in judgement. The affable manner that had fooled her into misplacing a top quality client with him smacked of the same polished charm that had fooled her into a miserable marriage ten years ago. She should have recognised it, been suspicious of it. Warning signals should have crawled down her spine.

'When I dictate a letter, I expect my secretary to type it word for word, each word spelled correctly,' Gordon Payne ranted on. 'I do not want her assuming she knows the English language better than me. If there is corrections to be made, *I* make them.'

Ashley held her tongue, mentally noting the two grammatical errors in that little speech. Here was another king-size ego who knew everything and could do no wrong! Ashley had been married to one for long enough to have experienced the God complex at close quarters. She had learnt there was no reasoning with it, no appeal that would pierce it, no way to get around it.

In her youthful naivety, Ashley had fallen blindly in love with Roger Harcourt. He had been handsome, always well-dressed, sophisticated in his tastes and strongly athletic, excelling in all competitive sports. Self-assurance had oozed from him, and during their early days together, Ashley had thought him utterly perfect.

Having drifted between divorced and disinterested parents for most of her teens, she had loved the way Roger took charge of everything and told her what was best for her to do. Ashley had interpreted that as proof of his caring for her. She'd had no perception of how tyrannical it could become.

She had thought she was getting love and strength and support and direction in her life when she had married Roger Harcourt.

She had certainly got direction.

She had had such a surfeit of direction from Roger, she doubted she would ever stomach the idea of marriage again. However difficult she sometimes found running her own life and being a single parent, it was still preferable to having her subordination taken as someone else's right.

Gordon Payne was now behaving as though she was subordinate to him, too. 'Run proper tests on these women in future. Don't believe their résumés,' he commanded. 'It's nothing but pretentious twaddle.'

As head of a home construction company—Painless Homes with Gordon Payne—and a member of the local shire council, he was a man of considerable standing in the community. Ashley had thought him a valuable business client, someone who would direct others to her agency if her service satisfied him. After hearing the dismissed secretary's story earlier this afternoon, she had decided then and there to cut him from her files, regardless of cost or consequences.

She was still inwardly fuming over the treatment that this pompous pain of a man had dished out to a young woman whom any sensible employer would cherish. Cheryn Kimball was too good for him. That was the problem.

Cheryn was not only highly qualified in all the areas Gordon Payne had demanded, she presented herself with style and polish and had a natural charm of manner that would endear her to most people. She had been traumatised, reduced to floods of tears by the unjust haranguing and arbitrary dismissal over doing what she believed to be her job.

'And I don't want a woman who talks back at me!' the monster ego raged.

That hit a particularly raw point with Ashley. Roger had felt he had the right to silence her by icily declaring, 'I am the head of this house!' What was she supposed to have been? The tail? The feet running after him all the time? She had discovered, too late, there were only one-way streets with Roger.

Ashley barely stopped herself from glowering at Gordon Payne. What he wanted was a mechanical robot programmed to toadying submission. Yes, master. At your service, master. Whatever you say, master.

The warm indulgence he had displayed towards his previous long-time secretary was explained in Cheryn's report. The woman had been mollycoddling him for the past twenty years. Even though she had retired, she had 'dropped in' at the office each day this week to 'break Cheryn in to the way dear Gordon likes things done,' and deliberately, jealously undermined Cheryn's confidence in her position and abilities.

Just like Roger's mother.

Ashley shuddered.

Roger's mother had considered herself a cut above everyone else since she was supposedly connected to some great line of landed gentry in Britain. Such pretensions had obviously contributed to Roger's sense of superiority. Her condescending manner had been a constant burr under Ashley's skin.

She hadn't wished Roger and his mother dead. She had made up her mind to divorce both of them. The fight for freedom had just begun when fate intervened and released her from the trauma of battling a custody case over William.

Of course, any reasonable person wouldn't have tried to drive across a bridge that was partly submerged by torrential floodwaters. Roger hadn't liked being beaten by anything. He and his mother had been swept away by a force bigger than both of them. They had probably drowned with a sense of outrage that such a thing could have happened.

Now here was this odious man reminding her of all she had put behind her. She wished she could wave a magic wand and give him a taste of servitude under someone like himself. Unfortunately her power of reprisal was strictly limited to a figurative kick out the door.

'I won't be paying your commission until you find me a suitable secretary,' was the predictable ultimatum. 'And I want someone in the office at nine o'clock tomorrow morning to get on with the work. A temporary will have to do until you come up with the right person.'

'I'm sorry you've been disappointed, Mr. Payne,' Ashley said coolly, 'but may I remind you that our contract was for me to supply you with three interviewees with the qualifications you listed. I did so. You chose Miss Kimball. You owe me five hundred dollars, and I expect to be paid.'

'You guaranteed satisfaction,' he answered angrily.

'You specified initiative as one of the qualities you required, Mr. Payne. Miss Kimball believed she was saving you the embarrassment of sending out grammatically incorrect letters. Many employers would value such care, knowledge and attention applied to their correspondence.'

That stung him. 'I tell you she got it wrong!' Gordon Payne's face developed angry red patches. 'When I specified initiative I meant for her to supply me with what I needed, when I needed it, without having to ask all the time. She failed that, too!'

'There is a difference between initiative and mind-reading, Mr. Payne. I do have a reader of tarot cards and a magician in my files, but I don't have any clairvoyants or mind-readers. Not amongst those seeking either permanent or temporary employment. I suggest you try some other agency.'

The red patches deepened to burning blotches.
He stood up, using his size to intimidate. He was
a bullish figure of a man, short-necked, broad-
shouldered, barrel-chested. His rather fleshy features were framed by crinkly brown hair, giving him
a deceptively boyish look for a man in his forties.
There was a mean glitter in his dark eyes.

'Don't get smart with me, Mrs. Harcourt,' he
snarled. 'I hold a position of influence in this town.
I could do you a lot of good.'

The threat that he could also do her a lot of
damage was left hanging, unspoken but clearly
implied.

Ashley was on the petite side, below average
height, delicately boned, slim-framed. She achieved
what she hoped was a mature and dignified stature
by wearing smartly tailored business suits and
pinning her long blond hair into a French pleat,
but her appearance was essentially dainty and
feminine.

Gordon Payne undoubtedly thought he could
make mincemeat out of her and eat her for
breakfast. What he didn't know was she was one
hundred per cent steel-proofed against being bullied
into anything she didn't want to do. If he'd looked
more closely he might have seen some sign of that
in the flintlike directness of her wide grey eyes.

She remained seated. This was her office, her
home, her castle, and no-one was going to shift her
from the position she had established for herself.
'I appreciate the offer, Mr. Payne,' she said calmly.

'I regret I can't return the favour. I've already done my best for you.'

He pressed the knuckles of one hand on her desk and leaned forward, his chin stuck out pugnaciously. 'You don't know what side your bread is buttered on, Mrs. Harcourt. You have wasted a great deal of my time, with no satisfactory result, and I expect you to make up for it.'

'How do you suggest I do that, Mr. Payne?'

'By supplying me with temporaries until you come up with a permanent who's satisfactory to my needs.'

'That was not part of our agreement,' she stated decisively. 'I have advised you that I cannot satisfy your new requirements and suggested you try another agency. Our business together is concluded, Mr. Payne.'

He glared at her as though he couldn't believe his ears.

Ashley pushed her chair back and rose smoothly to her feet. 'I'll see you out.'

'Like hell you will! I haven't finished with you yet.'

He stood his ground belligerently. Ashley had the distinct feeling he would block her path to the door if she skirted the desk and made a beeline for it. A physical confrontation would make him feel superior again. She stood completely still, hoping to defuse the aggression emanating from him.

'What more do you wish to say, Mr. Payne?' she enquired blandly.

'I can do you a lot of harm, Mrs. Harcourt,' he drawled, relishing the prospect of dealing in fear.

'Harm is a two-edged sword.'

'What can you do to me?' he jeered.

The smugness of the man goaded Ashley into a fighting reply. 'I have contacts, too, Mr. Payne. I could make sure that no-one will ever want to work for you personally again.'

He gave a derisive laugh. 'Money will take care of that.'

He was probably right. The power of money to corrupt even the highest principles was well proven. Ashley hated Gordon Payne's knowing use of it. The urge to knock him off his cocky perch gathered a compelling force as she remembered all the mean power games Roger had played on her.

Withholding money. Withholding use of the car. Demanding an account for everything she did while he didn't have to account for anything. Let Gordon Payne account for his behaviour, she thought blisteringly, losing all sense of discretion as she went on the attack.

'Money won't restore your reputation,' she asserted cuttingly. 'When Miss Kimball's story shows you up as a fool who doesn't know the English language—'

'I was right!'

The ugly humour was replaced by ugly fury. Ashley didn't care. She remorselessly drove the point home.

'No, Mr. Payne. You could not have been more wrong. You made a clown of yourself by defending the indefensible.'

Naked hatred glittered at her. 'Think yourself a balltearer, do you? One of those offensive, insulting females who are so envious of men, they'll do anything to pull them down.'

Ashley's chin lifted in lofty disdain of his opinion. 'You're certainly one of the men who justify the whole feminist movement.'

He sneered. 'I take it you're not a merry widow.' His gaze dropped to her breasts, her waist, her hips, his mouth curling salaciously. 'What you need is a man to get rid of your screwed-up frustrations.'

'A typically sexist statement to gloss over your own inadequacies, Mr. Payne.'

That thinned his fleshy lips and snapped his gaze back to hers. 'Well, we'll see who turns out to be inadequate, Mrs. Harcourt.' He picked up her favourite Lladro figurine from the desk. 'You have a fondness for clowns?'

She held her tongue, momentarily shocked by the malevolent gloating in his eyes. The wonderful clown he held in his hand was a masterpiece of expression, reflecting the sad ironies of life. Because she had stood up to Gordon Payne, it was about to be destroyed. She could see it coming, could do nothing to stop it and knew her adversary relished her helplessness. The realisation that she had been headstrong and foolish in challenging him came too late.

'I'll enjoy putting you at the centre of a circus, Mrs. Harcourt. I could start by having this home block of yours rezoned as wetlands. Then, of course, there's the licence for this agency. Needs investigation for legitimate practice. A visit from an industrial relations officer. A tax audit...' He lifted her figurine clown to shoulder height, ready to smash it down. 'This is what's going to happen to you....'

Ashley hadn't meant to cry out. She had resolved to suffer the inevitable in silent, contemptuous dignity. Yet an inarticulate croak of protest burst from her throat at the sheer, wanton destructiveness about to be enacted.

'You called, madam?' a very English voice enquired.

CHAPTER THREE

ASHLEY'S gaze was instantly drawn to the office door, which had been thrust open. Gordon Payne turned to look, too, the hand holding the Lladro clown lowering instinctively with the sudden appearance of a witness. They both stared in stunned silence at the totally unexpected vision of the man in the doorway.

He was not your ordinary, everyday person.

Ashley had never applied the word *elegant* to a man before, yet it leapt straight into her mind. Elegant, smashingly handsome and subtly dangerous.

He was tall and lean, beautifully dressed in a three-piece suit that had obviously been tailored for him, the smooth sheen of the blue-grey fabric shouting no expense spared. His white silk shirt had a buttoned down collar, and he wore a gorgeous tie in brilliant shades of blue.

His face was no less impressive, a squarish jawline, high cheekbones, straight nose, a perfectly moulded mouth, rakishly arched black eyebrows over the most dynamic blue eyes Ashley had ever seen. His black hair was thick and mostly straight. It was parted on the left side and swept across his high, wide forehead in a dipping wave.

In his right hand he carried a silver-knobbed black walking stick that tapered to a silver tip. He was not using it for support. He held it well below the knob, and his fingers had the long, agile look that suggested he could twiddle the cane much as Fred Astaire had in dancing routines. Or wield it very quickly as a lethal weapon.

He looked to be in his early thirties, but there was a world of knowledge in the eyes that scanned the scene he had thrust himself into with such timely éclat. He gave Ashley a quirky little smile, as though personally inviting her to relax and enjoy the moment. It was oddly intimate, forging an instant connection between them that embraced both understanding and acceptance that he was here for her.

It dazed Ashley. She had never experienced such a mental touch before. Not from a man. He didn't even know her. They had never met before. She was absolutely certain of that. Yet there was this strange feeling of recognition that he had always been meant to enter her life and play some vital part in it.

'Would you like me to see the gentleman out, madam?' he prompted with all the aplomb of a traditional British butler.

Ashley found her voice. 'Please,' she said gratefully, not caring from whence he had come, deeply relieved that he was offering to rid her of the menacing presence of an enemy she had recklessly made in unbridled and incautious anger.

'Who the devil are you?' Gordon Payne challenged sharply as her rescuer stepped into the room to carry out her request.

'Cliffton, sir,' came the lilting, blithe reply. He actually did twiddle the walking cane. In the flash of an eye it was suddenly resting in both his hands. 'The fortunes of the Harcourt family have been linked to the fortunes of my family for centuries.'

Centuries! Ashley's mind boggled at the claim. Apart from which, she wasn't a Harcourt. She had only married one, and not one that was a high recommendation of the name, either. Nevertheless, she was not about to spoil her white knight's pitch.

'It is both an honour and a pleasure to be of service once again,' he continued, smiling affably at Gordon Payne, who seemed mesmerised by Cliffton's approach. The way he was weaving the cane through his fingers with the dexterity of a magician was definitely having a hypnotic effect.

'May I, sir?' The cane was whipped under one arm like a shillelagh and both hands were out to relieve Gordon Payne of the Lladro clown. 'This piece is more for viewing than touching,' he advised with the air of an art connoisseur. 'If I put it back on its stand, I'm sure you'll appreciate its fine craftmanship better. There's a line and proportion to these things . . . there! You see?'

Somehow he'd deftly removed the figurine from Gordon Payne's grasp and set it on the desk, positioning it perfectly on its rectangular block and giving the clown's hat an affectionate pat as though it was an old friend.

'Now, sir, if you wouldn't mind, sir.' The cane was flicked into use again, pointing to the door. 'It is time to take your leave of Mrs. Harcourt. I'll see you on your way, sir.'

Ashley could almost feel Gordon Payne bristle as he recollected himself. Cliffton had snatched control from him, and he didn't like it. Not one bit. Yet some animal instinct must have warned him to avoid a trial of strength with the English stranger. He shot a last venomous glare at Ashley.

'You haven't heard the last of this.'

Then he swung on his heel and marched out, not waiting to be ushered or escorted to the front door of the house. Cliffton, however, dogged his steps, ensuring that he left without playing any malicious havoc with her possessions on his way. Ashley trailed after both of them, drawn to watch the end of a scene she now deeply regretted.

Making an enemy of Gordon Payne could rebound very badly on her. He had far more weapons than she did. It was self-defeating to start a fight she couldn't win. Hadn't Roger taught her that, over and over again? If the elegant Englishman had not arrived... Who was he, really? What was he? And why was he here?

She paused in the hallway just outside the office, noticing that he favoured his right leg, a slight limp, reason for the walking stick, yet he executed a smart, skipping sidestep that would have graced any dance floor, beating Gordon Payne to the front door with a deft panache that allowed him to open the door with a flourish.

'Good afternoon, sir,' he said with a respectful nod.

Gordon Payne stopped, stiffened and stared at him, flummoxed at being comprehensively out-manoeuvred. All he could manage was a crude snort in reply. Then he shook his shoulders as though dislodging a monkey on his back, propelled his feet forward again and made his exit from Ashley's house.

Harold Alistair Cliffton closed the door after him on a glorious high of triumphant satisfaction. He had out-butlered George, rescued the fair maiden and polished off the dragon. Maybe he had just found his true vocation in life. Being of service.

On the other hand, Harry suspected his exhilaration had much to do with being of service to Ashley Harcourt. He turned to face her again, aware that she had followed to watch the curtain line of his masterly performance.

The photographs had not done her justice. They hadn't captured the essence of Ashley Harcourt at all. Harry couldn't quite put words to that essence, but it was something that sparked an instant response in him, an excitement, a sense of meeting someone special.

The moment their eyes had met . . . zing! Like an electric charge. He had felt truly alive again. Grey eyes, completely unlike Pen's soft brown, yet there

was something in them that called to him, just as
Pen's had. Perhaps a sureness of who and what she
was, a belief in herself.

He wanted to know more about her. He wanted
to know everything about her. The idea came to
him in an inspired flash. Why not keep on playing
the butler? It wasn't at all difficult. In fact, he was
enjoying the role immensely. It also had a great
many advantages.

A butler was in the happy position of always
being on hand. Installed under the same roof as
Ashley Harcourt, he could get to know her very
well, indeed. Harry rather relished the idea of
putting Ashley to bed at night and waking her up
in the morning with steaming hot . . . coffee. Like
George, he'd be Father Confessor, confidant, ad-
viser, helpmate, on the spot to test the waters for
other possible attachments.

It allowed him to thoroughly investigate the situation for getting George an heir for Springfield
Manor. This could become an extraordinary ex-
ploit that would add to the legends already sur-
rounding his illustrious family—how Harry brought
the Black Sheep strain back into the fold!

Alternatively, it might eventuate that young
William need not fill the position of heir at all. His
mother was beginning to inspire a lively set of other
possibilities. He wondered how long her silky
blonde hair was when unpinned and flowing free.
On a pillow.

Ashley remained rooted near the door into the office, studying the extraordinary man who had erupted into her life with sensational effect. Not only with Gordon Payne. She was acutely conscious of a sense of tingly anticipation, as though she knew intuitively that his startling actions were only the forerunner of more startling actions.

He aimed another quirky smile at her, his bright blue eyes twinkling with unholy mischief. He gestured to the door and commented, 'I thought him a mite touchy.'

Ashley couldn't help being amused. To describe Gordon Payne as *touchy* seemed a masterful understatement. 'I shouldn't have lost my temper,' she said with a rueful grimace.

Cliffton looked sympathetic. 'Touchy people are often aggressive and unpredictable.'

'It was stupid of me.'

One eyebrow lifted in considering assessment. 'Perhaps a tad impetuous, madam. Still, there is an arguable case for throwing caution to the winds and letting fly. Gets a load off the chest, so to speak.'

Ashley could barely stop her mouth from twitching. He was so attractive, so...debonair. Another word she had never applied to a man! Not in real life. Her mind drifted to the Scarlet Pimpernel and she hastily pulled it back to a somewhat frayed level of common sense. Don't forget *dangerous*, she cautioned herself.

'What would you have done if he hadn't let you take the Lladro clown?' she asked.

'Broken his wrist most likely,' came the imperturbable reply. 'Brings to mind the incident with Good Queen Bess,' he mused. 'My ancestor, Hugo, broke the wrist of the Spanish ambassador who presented a gift to the queen, then tried to take it back when she dismissed his king's request.'

Ashley's mind slipped again. Spanning centuries seemed quite normal with Cliffton. 'If you'd done that,' she said, trying to latch onto something practical, 'the figurine would have fallen and broken.'

He grinned. 'Never missed a catch at first slip. I used to play in the first eleven cricket team at school.'

Ashley had no trouble imagining Cliffton being first at a lot of things. But he didn't seem conceited about it. Nor did he emit an air of superiority. Not like Roger. Whatever his abilities, he simply accepted them as completely natural.

Which brought her back to the questions that needed answering. She couldn't let this discussion run on as though they were old and intimate friends. Common sense insisted she had to establish who this man was and what he was doing here.

'I could be a mite touchy, too,' she warned. 'About having a stranger invade my home and eavesdrop on a private conversation.'

'No, no, madam. I would not be so ill-mannered as to enter anyone's home uninvited. Master William let me in.'

'Master William?' She wondered how her nine-year-old son had reacted to being addressed in such a fashion!

'He was playing cricket next door. Has the makings of a fine batsman,' Cliffton remarked admiringly. 'He played a superb hook shot, which I happened to catch before it hit the windscreen of the Daimler that was parked at the kerb outside your house.'

'Oh, Lord!' Ashley breathed, relieved that Gordon Payne didn't have damage to his car to add to his list of grudges against her.

'I explained to Master William that I was on a mission from England and needed to call on you. He told me to wait in the lounge until you were ready to receive me. I was about to enter that room, as instructed by Master William, when a highly unpleasant voice penetrated to the hallway, listing a most unseemly set of threats.'

He put on a mournful face. 'I do apologise for eavesdropping, madam. Most reprehensible of me. It reminded me of a situation that confronted my ancestor, Stafford, with the sheriff of Nottingham over a man called Hood. But right won out in the end, madam. We Clifftons have a way of making things turn out right in the end.'

Ashley was still trying to swallow that story as he went on.

'I must also confess to falling into a trance of admiration at the spirited way you took the gentleman to task. Not a nice gentleman at all, I must say. Then when you cried out...' He shrugged appealingly. 'I thought I could be of service to you.'

'Yes. You were. Thank you.' His voice was wonderfully musical, quite enthralling to listen to. 'What mission?' Ashley asked belatedly. 'Who are you?'

'Butler to the English branch of the Harcourt family.'

He really *was* a butler!

'A hereditary position, madam. I come as an emissary from the last of your Harcourt relatives in Britain.'

Ashley stiffened, snapping herself out of her bemused daze. Roger's mother must have been telling the truth about being connected to a line of landed gentry in England. Although that still did not give her the right to have adopted the attitude of being better than anyone else.

It was an attitude that won no sympathy whatsoever from Ashley. She herself might bear the Harcourt name, keeping it because it was her son's birthright, but it held no sway with her. The reverse, in fact.

'In the current circumstances, your son, William, is the master of Springfield Manor's only heir, madam, and he would like you both to take up residence at the manor, his country home. I am assigned to help you settle your affairs and expedite your journey to England.'

Typically high-handed, Ashley thought, her backbone getting stiffer by the second. No Harcourt was going to tell her what to do with her life. She had had her fill of that, thank you very much.

Cliffton gave her a smile of such charm the stiffening almost came undone. 'For however long it takes to accomplish that, madam, I am to stay here as your butler,' he declared winningly, 'to serve you and Master William as you will.'

CHAPTER FOUR

FOR as long as it takes ...

What monstrous arrogance!

Ashley saw red for several seconds before the brilliant blue eyes of the butler drove the red away. Not Cliffton's arrogance, of course. He was merely carrying out his master's instructions. Although why a man like Cliffton could be content to serve a Harcourt... Imbued with the English class system and centuries of tradition, she supposed, excusing him on the grounds of having been brainwashed from birth.

One thing was certain. She was not going to be carted off to England and suffer the condescension of the gentry installed in Springfield Manor. If William was an heir, he could wait until his inheritance was free and clear of every other Harcourt before considering what it involved and what was best done about it.

In the meantime, Ashley had to decide what to do about Cliffton. Outright rejection of his mission probably meant he would have to return to England to report failure, and she wouldn't see him again unless she followed. That scenario had no appeal whatsoever.

Ashley had never felt so drawn to know more about a person. Cliffton was, without a doubt, the most fascinating man she had ever met, and she didn't want him to drop out of her life before she had the chance to...well, explore possibilities.

He was special. Far too special to be a butler. Maybe a short sojourn in Australia might show him other ways of life that could be far more rewarding than being a butler, yet she could probably only keep him with her if she appeared to be considering the proposition, perhaps needing some persuasion from him to make up her mind.

For as long as it takes...

That suddenly became a highly seductive little phrase.

Taking her years with Roger and his mother into account, Ashley had no problem in reasoning that the Harcourt family did owe her some recompense, and Cliffton clearly didn't mind being her butler for a while. He would be very handy to have around if Gordon Payne decided to carry through on his threats. That could be classed as helping to settle her affairs.

In fact, she could find lots of business that would need settling before she could even consider uprooting their lives and going to England with William. What about William's schooling and leaving all his friends behind? There were many difficulties and obstacles to overcome, and in all good faith, serious matters that would prove quite impossible to resolve in the end. Cliffton would eventually come to see that, and no blame would attach to him for failing to accomplish what was expected of him.

It was only fair to give his mission a chance at succeeding.

Even if it was mission impossible.

Ashley had to smother a huge upsurge of elation at this highly satisfactory conclusion. She lifted a hand to her temple, rubbing at it in a distracted fashion, covering any telltale expression in her eyes as she said somewhat faintly, 'This is all a bit of a shock.'

'Forgive me, madam.' Cliffton was at her side in a flash, gently steering her into the lounge. 'Thoughtless of me to regale you with all this when you've had no time to recover from that nasty encounter. Such incidents do sap one's energy.'

There was absolutely nothing wrong with Ashley's energy. Cliffton's light grasp on her elbow gave it a remarkable boost. She caught a whiff of some tantalising aftershave lotion and wished she was wearing perfume and a more alluring outfit than a business suit. One of the wonderful chiffon gowns that Ginger Rogers used to wear floated into her mind.

At Cliffton's direction she sank into an armchair. He whizzed a footstool under her feet, plumped up a cushion and slid it behind her back for extra comfort, pulled out one of her set of three occasional tables and placed it within easy hand's

reach, then straightened up and smiled benevolent-
ly at her.

'A cup of tea is always soothing, madam. Or
perhaps, since it's after five o'clock, a glass of
sherry? Sherry is more fortifying. On the other
hand, a gin and tonic can have an elevating effect.
I am at your service, madam. If you'll tell me what
you'd like...'

Ashley had a mad urge to ask for slippers and a
pipe! She sternly reminded herself this was not a
game to Cliffton. He was doing what he was trained
to do, and her best course, at the moment, was to
accept his offer graciously. 'A cup of tea would be
lovely. Thank you,' she said with a grateful smile.

He left her before Ashley thought to give directions to the kitchen and where to find everything.
Further consideration assured her that Cliffton
would have no difficulty finding his way around.
This was hardly a butler-size house. The kitchen
was at the end of the hallway and was of a fairly
standard design. Making a cup of tea did not
present a problem.

Finding living quarters for Cliffton did.

Although there were three bedrooms, the third
was used for storing William's sporting equipment
and housing whatever hobbies had captured his
interest. Model aeroplanes and ships took up most
of the shelf space, and a work table was currently
covered in miniature soldiers, which he was painting
in preparation for a replay of the Napoleonic Wars.

A divan bed, shoved against one of the walls, and no cupboard space at all, did not constitute a suitable room for a guest who would be staying longer than overnight. The spare twin bed in William's room didn't present attractive accommodation, either. Which left her room, and it was utterly ridiculous for her to move out and offer the master bedroom to the butler.

It suddenly struck her that she should have asked Cliffton for some credentials instead of accepting his story at face value. The man was a stranger, for heaven's sake! His sheer panache had bamboozled her into being totally unbusinesslike. She had better correct that as soon as he reappeared. Or maybe she should be checking on him right now instead of letting him have the run of the house. What if...

The front door banged open and William came pelting inside, pulling himself to a halt as he caught sight of Ashley through the doorway into the lounge. He looked flushed and excited.

'Hey, Mum! Where's...' He stopped as he took in the cushion at her back and her feet on the footstool. 'Have you twisted your ankle or something?'

'I'm just relaxing,' she said, feeling a flush sweeping up her neck as though she'd been caught in a compromising position.

'Oh! Okay!' William dismissed the incomprehensible in favour of imparting the exciting news that had brought him in. 'You should see the great car Mr. Cliffton came in. It's a smashing Rolls

Royce. The chauffeur said it's a 1987 Silver Spirit. How about that?'

Ashley's mind boggled again. The wayward thought came to her that it would have put Gordon Payne's nose further out of joint at seeing a Rolls Royce outshining his Daimler. Not to mention a chauffeur!

Fortunately William didn't require a reply. Cliffton arrived on the scene bearing the silver tray and tea service that Roger's mother had given to them as a wedding gift.

'What are you doing with that?' William asked bluntly, as astonished as Ashley was. Cliffton must have dug it out of the bottom of the dresser where it had resided untouched, apart from cleaning, for many years.

'Your mother is feeling poorly. I am serving her tea,' Cliffton replied with unruffled decorum.

William looked wide-eyed at Ashley. 'Are you sick?'

Her cheeks blossomed with hot colour. 'I'm recovering fast,' she answered.

'You don't need me then?' William asked.

'No. I'll be fine in a minute.'

'Right!' William looked relieved and turned quickly to the butler. 'You'll be staying for a bit, Mr. Cliffton?'

'Yes. I'll be staying as long as—'

'Great!' William cut him off and offered his most appealing face. 'Would you mind if my friends had a turn at sitting in your car? They wouldn't hurt anything. The chauffeur could let them in and out. I promise they'll be good.'

Cliffton set the tray down on the occasional table and eyed William consideringly. 'How much do you intend to charge?'

William grinned at the quick understanding. 'Only ten cents each. Ten dollars with a photo. Can I borrow your Polaroid camera, Mum?'

'Ten dollars!' Ashley gasped in shock.

'Think, Mum,' her son advocated earnestly. 'This will be a once-in-a-lifetime photograph, a memory they'll be able to pull out of a photo album in years to come to show they really did drive a Rolls Royce. A photo of that value can't go cheaply.'

William always seemed to have a line of inarguable logic for what he wanted to do. 'You said sit in it!' Ashley sharply reminded him.

'If they sit behind the driving wheel it'll look as though they're driving it. I won't actually let them,' he assured Cliffton.

'I am very impressed with the sales pitch,' Cliffton said admiringly.

'So you see, Mum?' William pressed. 'I have to have the camera.'

'William, you haven't received permission about the car, and I don't think...'

'Permission granted,' Cliffton chimed in, his blue eyes twinkling approval.

'The camera, Mum?'

Two against one defeated her. 'Yes.' She sighed, her need to settle various matters with Cliffton more urgent and important than arguing with William over his schemes for augmenting his pocket money.

'Thanks, Mum. Thanks a lot, Mr. Cliffton. I think I'm going to like you.'

He was off like a flash to fleece his friends' pockets.

'Weak or strong, madam?'

Cliffton had the silver teapot poised, ready to pour.

'However it comes,' Ashley answered distractedly. 'You came here in a chauffeured Rolls Royce?'

'It is the customary mode of transport at Springfield Manor, madam. The master wants you to know you'll be given every comfort. Milk, madam?'

'Yes. But surely you didn't bring a Rolls Royce with you from England. Did you?' she added, struck with the feeling that anything was possible with this man.

'I acquired it when I arrived in Sydney, madam. Sugar?'

'No, thank you. I don't think . . .' Ashley floundered, appalled at the cost of a mission that would certainly—well, almost certainly—be futile. 'You really shouldn't be spending so much on a campaign that might come to nothing,' she burst out. 'A Rolls Royce, for heaven's sake! This seems to be getting quite out of hand.'

'How else can you be shown what to expect, madam?' Cliffton enquired reasonably. 'You haven't tried it yet,' he pointed out. 'I think you'll get to like it. It's quite pleasant and tends to get addictive.'

She was not going to be seduced by a Rolls Royce into becoming a dependant at Springfield Manor. 'I do not need a Rolls Royce,' she stated emphatically. 'And what's more, Cliffton, this smacks of trying to buy my acquiescence to what you want.'

'It is always interesting to test resistance to its limits, madam,' he said with an air of taking up an irresistible challenge.

'Why on earth should you do such a thing?' she demanded. Surely he was taking this mission too far.

'It's in the spirit of my more adventurous forebears who would never take no for an answer.'

Irrepressible, Ashley thought, beginning to appreciate Gordon Payne's perspicacity in retreating from Cliffton rather than taking him on. What could one do in the face of such an unsquashable spirit? And really, did she want to say no to Cliffton? It was only the ultimate no to the Harcourt family that she would have to impress upon him.

'Well, I won't be held responsible for what you spend,' Ashley stated unequivocally.

'The responsibility is entirely mine,' Cliffton agreed. 'Your tea, madam.'

'Oh! Thank you.' In a Royal Crown Derby fine bone china teacup, no less, inherited from her mother-in-law. How much fossicking had Cliffton done in her kitchen? Ashley's whirling mind spun to other concerns, like the possible undermining of her authority with William. 'I don't think you should have let William use the car as a...as a—'

'Money-making venture?' Cliffton supplied.

'Yes.'

'If I may say so, madam, one should never stifle enterprise. In my youth I used to organise frog races. With his entrepreneurial talents, Master William will undoubtedly—'

'Stop!'

'I beg your pardon, madam?'

'You can't call him master. I won't have it.' The last thing she wanted was for William to start thinking he was of a superior breed to anyone else. 'There are no masters in Australia. There are only people, Cliffton,' she added earnestly. 'You must understand that or you won't do any good here.'

'Thank you for your advice, madam,' he said gravely. 'Is there anything else I should know so as not to give offence?'

'I'm not a madam. Madams are people who run brothels.'

'Oh!' The quirky little smile twitched at the corners of his mouth. 'Then that's clearly inappropriate. I shall call you milady.'

'I'm not your lady.' Ashley managed not to say, 'Yet.'

'Mrs. Harcourt?'

She didn't want to be reminded of her marriage to Roger, either, but perhaps it wasn't appropriate to ask Cliffton to call her Ashley at this point. It could wait until she knew him better. She nodded her assent to the name and sipped her tea, trying desperately to collect her thoughts into a properly ordered pattern.

Events seemed to be tumbling over themselves, not giving her time to sort through what needed to be done. And it didn't help to have Cliffton hovering over her enquiringly. Not only were the beautiful blue depths of his eyes enough for her wits to drown in, she seemed to be getting a fixation on the tantalising little tilts and curves of his mouth. She hadn't thought about being kissed by a man for quite a while. The provocative question arose.... Did butlers help put their mistresses to bed?

Ashley was shocked at herself, but a perverse little voice whispered that it had been over six years and she was as normal as the next woman in wanting an exciting relationship with a man, so it was perfectly all right to fantasise what it might be like. Especially with a man of Cliffton's unusual and extraordinary qualities. In fact, she wouldn't be normal if she didn't.

It took an enormous effort of will to drag her mind back to practical matters. 'I think you should show me some credentials, Cliffton,' she said soberly. 'After all, it's asking a lot for me to accept what you're saying off the cuff, so to speak.'

'Quite right! I have the investigative report tracing the family line to young William in my luggage. I shall ask the chauffeur to fetch it in as soon as the photograph session is over. In the meantime, will my passport suffice as a means of identification?'

He removed it from an inner pocket in his suit coat and offered it to her. Ashley put down her teacup, intent on examining whatever solid information she could get about him. It was certainly a British passport, and the photograph unmistakably identified him as Harold Alistair Cliffton. A *very* English name, Ashley thought.

'Harold,' she mused out loud, thinking it didn't really fit him.

'Nobody ever calls me by that name, Mrs. Harcourt,' came the decisive correction. 'Harold is merely a remnant from the Battle of Hastings.'

Yes, it did belong in the realms of history, Ashley privately agreed. She supposed using the surname Cliffton was traditional for a butler, and she shouldn't mess with that formality. Not yet, anyway. However, her curiosity was piqued.

'What about when you were a boy?' she probed.

'I was always Harry.'

Harry. That was better. More lively. She could imagine a Harry organising frog races. A Harry could definitely be as debonair as Fred Astaire.

His date of birth gave her his age. Thirty-three. She suddenly had an awful thought. 'Are you married, Cliffton?'

'No. Unhappily, the woman to whom I was deeply attached died some years ago,' he said sadly. 'As I have no current ties, it was no hardship for me to come away on this mission.'

Free and clear. Ashley was intensely relieved to hear it. Although it did sound as though he had once been very much in love. But that was years ago. And it did demonstrate he was capable of loving someone other than himself, which was all to the good.

'This gives your birthplace as Springfield Manor,' she observed inquiringly.

'As I explained, I hold a hereditary position. Generations of my family have been born at Springfield Manor.'

That wasn't so good. It meant Cliffton had deep roots there. Maybe she shouldn't start something that had little hope of a happy ending. However tempting it was to prolong an involvement with him, it wasn't exactly honest to let him think she was prepared to fall in with the plans made for her and accompany him to Springfield Manor.

Her usual sense of integrity reared its head. She handed him his passport and mustered up the strength to meet his gaze with steady eyes. 'You have rather sprung this on me, Cliffton. I'm sure you think that William and I will be better off living at Springfield Manor, but I've got to tell you that giving up a life of independence goes very much against my grain. It also goes against my grain that I'm being placed in a position of obligation without my consent. I don't like being beholden to anyone for anything.'

To Ashley's surprise, Cliffton looked pleased at this declaration. His eyes positively danced approval. 'I quite understand, Mrs. Harcourt. There is nothing worse than a burden of obligation or the sense of not having a free choice. Believe me, it is the last thing I would put upon you. I merely offer. You decide what you want.'

Put like that, Ashley could find no objection to tasting the waters without committing herself to the whole deal.

'As I see the situation,' Cliffton went on persuasively, 'everyone has personal needs. It is a matter of working out whether or not yours can be accommodated to your satisfaction. I appreciate that this will take time.'

'Yes,' she quickly agreed. 'It will take time. It could be years.'

'As long as it takes,' he reasserted with bland unconcern.

'It may never be worked out to my satisfaction,' she warned.

'One can but give it fair trial.'

'As long as that's understood.'

'Absolutely.'

Integrity satisfied, Ashley decided she had to tackle the accommodation question. 'This isn't a big house, Cliffton.'

'It appears to be very cosy and comfortable and practical. You have every reason to be proud of it.'

'Thank you. I wasn't apologising for its lack of grandeur,' she said dryly. 'I was about to point out we don't have a lot of room. Are you prepared to live with less than you're obviously accustomed to?'

'I was a boy scout. A tent in the backyard will suffice,' came the blithe reply.

'No, no, we don't have to go that far.' He was clearly bent on staying with her, no matter what, and Ashley found herself feeling highly gratified by the fact. 'There is a spare bedroom but it is small and rather cluttered. I think you'll have to negotiate with William over what stays and what goes to make room for your things. It's rather complicated with a miniature army of soldiers that are in the process of being painted.'

He grinned. 'I can see your William is a lad after my own heart, Mrs. Harcourt. Perhaps I can help him set up a battlefield. I once did a papier-mâché model for the Battle of Waterloo. One of my ancestors was a key figure in the defence of Hougoumont against the French.'

Cliffton could become the father figure William had been missing all these years, Ashley thought hopefully.

Or was he a soul mate?

Despite Cliffton's mastery of decorum, there was definitely a glint of mischief in his eyes that suggested something wild and wicked lived behind the pose of proper propriety. He was obviously in tune with William's entrepreneurial skills. A hereditary butler was probably in the perfect position to be an opportunist with both his master and his master's guests. Ashley suspected that Cliffton did very well for himself.

Look at his clothes. And the Rolls Royce. Maybe an egalitarian society wouldn't suit him nearly so well. On the other hand, if he was prepared to camp in a tent in the backyard, he was nothing if not flexible.

Since there seemed to be no wrong in accepting him into the house as her butler, at least on a temporary basis, Ashley made her decision with a clear conscience and an exciting sense of adventure. Having a butler would undoubtedly be an interesting and novel experience. When the butler was Cliffton, well, who knew what might happen?

She smiled. 'Is there anything you wish to settle with me before bringing in your luggage?'

He smiled back. 'I believe we've covered everything of present importance, Mrs. Harcourt.'

Ashley could feel his satisfaction and was highly conscious of her own. A two-way street, she thought with growing pleasure.

'Then welcome to our home, Cliffton.'

'Thank you, Mrs. Harcourt.'

How that name grated on Ashley's ears!

'Please be assured I will serve you as best I can until everything is resolved,' he continued.

Happily, she hoped.

'In the meantime, I shall go and survey the sleeping quarters and come to an accommodation with William.'

Ashley came to another decision. 'There is one other thing. In Australia it's quite customary for both employer and employee to call each other by their first names. I'm not even your employer. And since we'll be living in constant proximity, I think it would be more appropriate if I call you Harry and you call me Ashley. It won't, uh, interfere with your duties, and I'll feel more comfortable with it. If you don't mind.'

'Your comfort is my duty,' he replied, giving her a dazzling smile. 'Ashley it is.'

'Thank you, Harry.'

'My pleasure.'

He left her to savour her pleasure, and it was very warm, warmer than anything Ashley had felt for a long, long time.

CHAPTER FIVE

NO SOONER had William's friends scattered home for their evening meal than Ashley was faced with some of the wider consequences of accepting Harry into her household.

The telephone rang.

Ashley was slow in answering the call. Harry had insisted on preparing dinner, and William, most uncharacteristically, was helping him. She had slipped upstairs to change out of her business suit and freshen up generally for the evening ahead. By the time she emerged from the bathroom and picked up the receiver in her bedroom, Harry was already on the kitchen extension.

'The Harcourt residence. May I enquire who's calling, please?'

Ashley held her tongue, curious to know how Harry would deal with the caller.

'It's Olivia Stanton. Dylan's mother.'

Ashley grimaced. Olivia was the president of the Parents' and Citizens' Association at William's school, and she had a habit of minding everybody else's business. Her snippy tone indicated a complaint was about to be voiced.

'How do you do, Mrs. Stanton?' Harry's English accent suddenly developed a very plummy tone. 'How may I help you?'

A slight pause. 'To whom am I speaking?'

'My name is Cliffton. I am Mrs. Harcourt's butler.'

'Butler!'

Her astonishment was unmistakable. A butler was a most uncommon personage in Australia, let alone in the Central Coast area of Wamberal. Probably the prime minister or the governor-general had one for official receptions, but Ashley couldn't even vouch for that.

'Did you say butler?'

Olivia Stanton was clearly rocked off her set course.

'I did, Mrs. Stanton.'

'What is Ashley Harcourt doing with a butler? I didn't know she could afford one.'

The rhetorical question, followed by the comment on her financial position, made Ashley realise that Harry's arrival in her life would give rise to enormous speculation and gossip in the neighbourhood. It was a measure of her enthralment with Harry that Ashley found she wasn't overly troubled by this prospect. Let them say what they liked. And they'd certainly do that when they saw him! Her course was set. She was going to keep the butler, no matter what!

'I believe my services are of value, Mrs. Stanton,' Harry answered silkily.

'Well, it is unusual.' Olivia justified her rudeness.

'Perhaps it will start a fashion, Mrs. Stanton. Mrs. Harcourt does run an employment agency.'

Ashley grinned. That was a clever stroke.

'Are you connected to the Rolls Royce that's involved in these outrageous photographs?'

Ashley rolled her eyes, knowing full well that another of William's schemes was coming home to roost.

'It comes with me, Mrs. Stanton,' Harry answered smoothly.

He had solved the problem of accommodating the chauffeur and getting the car off the street by sending them both to a local motel. He dismissed the cost as though it was nothing, assuring Ashley once again that she would not be held financially liable for what he did in pursuit of a successful outcome to his mission.

And the mission had been verified. Harry had shown her the branch of Roger's family tree that had originated from England. It was amazing that so many people had died off, leaving only William as the last of this specific blood line.

'Do you know what use William made of your car this afternoon?' Olivia demanded testily.

'Yes, I do.'

'Are you aware that he is charging ten dollars for the photographs he took?'

'As I understand it, there is no obligation to buy, Mrs. Stanton. If you can't afford the price—'

'I didn't say that.'

'The boys were very happy about the chance of being photographed at the wheel of a Rolls Royce, but if you want Dylan to be unhappy—'

'I didn't say that, either.'

'A once-in-a-lifetime occurrence, Mrs. Stanton, is not something to be belittled. You are, of course, entitled to disagree. I believe William can bear the cost of Dylan being left out of the photographs—'

'I don't want him left out,' Olivia cried, drowning in the string of logic that had flowed from Harry's silver tongue.

'Of course not, Mrs. Stanton. No mother would want her son left out of something so special. Shall I tell William to put Dylan's photograph in the sold pile?'

A died-in-the-wool accomplice, Ashley thought, bemused and amused by his dexterity in handling the most difficult people.

'Yes,' Olivia surrendered weakly.

'Thank you, Mrs. Stanton. Is there anything else? A message for Mrs. Harcourt?'

'No.'

'Then thank you for calling, Mrs. Stanton.'

Killed off with politeness, Ashley thought, as she heard the line disconnect. On the other hand, Olivia was probably dying to get a free line so she could spread the news of Ashley's acquisition of a butler who came with a chauffeured Rolls Royce. It would certainly add a bit of spice to her reputation as a businesswoman.

Fortunately it was no longer a scandalous matter for a man and woman to be living under the same roof together without benefit of marriage. Ashley had no doubt that most of her friends and acquaintances would take the attitude, 'Good luck to you!' while they tried to stifle their envy.

However, she did need to warn Harry not to say anything about their connection to Springfield Manor. That was their private business. Apart from which, it would spoil everything. She didn't want to think about it herself. She simply wanted to enjoy having Harry fix things for her as he'd been doing so beautifully ever since he had arrived.

As on most January days, the heat of summer lingered long into the evening. Ashley zipped herself into her favourite sundress. It was casual enough not to look too dressed up. The polished cotton was cool and the pretty pink and green floral print suited her colouring. The bodice was fitted, with shoestring straps over her shoulders. The full circular skirt always made her feel feminine.

Normally, she would unpin her hair at this time, brush it out and clip it into a high ponytail to keep it off her neck. Practical it might be, but it didn't look elegant. She effected a more sophisticated casual look by winding it into a loose knot on top of her head. Several strands artfully escaped.

She dabbed on some Beautiful perfume, applied a silvery pink lipstick, slid her feet into strappy white sandals and hoped that Harry would find her more than passably attractive.

The staircase led down to the family room, which was separated from the kitchen by a wide working counter that also served as a breakfast bar. She heard William peppering Harry with questions as she started down. Something about ghosts. William was fascinated with the supernatural.

Harry, however, lost the thread of their conversation as Ashley came into full view on the staircase. His hands stopped tossing the salad he had mixed in a bowl. He watched her descend as though transfixed by her grace and beauty. At least, Ashley hoped that was what was captivating him, and he wasn't simply surprised by the change in her appearance. It was much more heart-lifting to fantasise that he was seeing a woman who attracted and intrigued him.

She was conscious of the full skirt swishing around her bare legs as she descended step by step, conscious of silky strands of hair brushing against the smooth golden tan of her bare shoulders, more intensely conscious of her sexuality than she had been in so many years she had forgotten how powerful the feeling could be. She had given up believing she would meet a man who would trigger such a response in her.

She could feel her whole body glowing under the interest in Harry's eyes, an interest that clearly sizzled with sensual signals as it enveloped all of her, from the loosely draped topknot of her hair to the swell of her full breasts encased in the tightly fitting bodice to the emphasised curve of waist and hips to the dainty slimness of her ankles. All her instincts picked up the knowledge that he found her desirable, and she revelled in the certainty that the strong attraction she felt was not one-sided.

'Oh, hi, Mum! You've interrupted a great story!' William informed her, seeing no reason for the halt in his entertainment.

'Your mother has first claim on my attention, William,' Harry said, quietly but firmly putting her son in his place, his gaze not even slightly wavering from her. His eyes seemed to bathe her with warm pleasure as he added, 'Good evening, Ashley.'

The formal greeting didn't feel like a formality at all. It felt like a promise of wonderful things to come. The gateway to possibilities was open. 'Good evening, Harry,' she returned, giving him a smile that welcomed him to her world.

He had discarded his suit coat and rolled up his shirt sleeves. Ashley noticed that his shoulders didn't need any padding and his forearms were strongly muscular. He was still lean and elegant, but she added physical power to his other attributes, and had little doubt he could fight with more than words, if need be. Harry Cliffton, she decided, was a man with many sides to him. Ashley wanted to discover all of them.

The telephone rang again.

William sighed at this further interruption to the subject that interested him.

Harry took the receiver from the wall phone above the counter. 'The Harcourt residence...'

Ashley walked to the other side of the counter as Harry listened to the person on the other end of the line.

'Just a moment, Mrs. Stanton. I'll see if Mrs. Harcourt is available.'

He held the receiver to his chest as his eyes queried hers.

'Fusspot,' William muttered.

Ashley frowned at him, not approving of disrespect to his elders, although privately she was inclined to agree with him. Olivia Stanton was not her favourite person. Nevertheless, she was a neighbour and the mother of one of William's friends, and it was political to keep on her good side if she wasn't demanding too much. She nodded to Harry and held out her hand.

'Mrs. Harcourt will take your call now, Mrs. Stanton,' Harry announced with marvellous aplomb before passing the receiver to her.

'Olivia—' Ashley tried to inject interest into her voice.

'Ten dollars is a lot of money for one photo, Ashley.'

Olivia hated losing a battle. Flummoxed by Harry, she had obviously decided to shift to another opponent. Having been shown the way to defeat the woman, Ashley took a leaf out of Harry's book.

'What price do you put on your son's smile, Olivia?' she asked sweetly.

Harry's eyes danced pure delight at her. Ashley's heart flipped.

'All right. It's very cheap then,' Olivia conceded, surprising Ashley with such a quick dismissal of the grievance. 'What I was wondering, Ashley, was whether... I'm having my annual neighbourhood party in a week's time....'

This was news to Ashley. She hadn't received an invitation.

'I was wondering if you'd lend me your butler and Rolls Royce for the evening?'

Olivia Stanton had the hide of a rhinoceros. It did make her effective at fundraising for the school, which also fed her self-importance, but this was pure one-upmanship on a personal level, no connection whatsoever with public do-gooding.

'I'm afraid Cliffton is not a lendable commodity, Olivia,' she replied, barely keeping a sardonic edge out of her voice. 'It certainly couldn't be done without his consent. A butler is not a slave, you know. Butlering is a highly respected profession that requires absolute savoir faire and perfect organizational skills, not to mention an impeccable reputation, since he holds such a position of trust.'

Ashley couldn't stop her eyes from flirting wickedly with Harry's as she described his position. She paused for a moment to give Olivia time to swallow all she'd said, then obligingly added, 'I will ask him, if you like.'

'Well, there's no harm in asking, I always say,' came the bull-headed reply.

'Then please excuse me a moment, Olivia. I'll put it to him.' She held her hand over the receiver and grinned at Harry. 'You're already in demand. Olivia Stanton would like to borrow your invaluable services for her neighbourhood party.'

'Don't do it,' William said. 'She's full of herself as it is.'

'That's quite enough, William,' Ashley reproved sharply. He was getting altogether too bold in his opinions. And indiscreet!

'The duties of my profession demand that I stay with you,' Harry stated virtuously.

'Quite so,' Ashley agreed with mock seriousness. She lifted the receiver to her ear again. 'I'm sorry, Olivia. I'm afraid butler ethics prohibit the lending of a butler. He has to stay with me.'

'Of course, I'd forgotten about that, but perhaps you and he would like to attend as guests.'

Sly vixen, Ashley thought, determined not to fall into that trap. Having established Harry as her butler, to turn up with him as her escort would be tantamount to handing Olivia Stanton evidence that all was not as it should be. After assuming a proper correctness about Harry's professional life, Ashley was not about to cross lines. Besides, she wanted to keep Harry to herself.

'I'm quite sure Cliffton will have me ready for your party in time,' she said with airy confidence. 'When did you say it was?'

'Eight o'clock next Saturday.'

'Lovely! He might even drive me up in the Rolls and park it outside your house for an hour or two.' That would lend some of the status that Olivia desired for her party. 'As it's only a short distance away, I don't think Cliffton will mind taking me there and walking home. Thank you for inviting me, Olivia. I must go now. Bye.'

She hung up on the meddlesome woman and raised her eyebrows in appeal to Harry. 'Would you mind?'

He gave a deeply meaningful look. 'I'll give you anything you want, Ashley.'

It sent a little thrill of pleasure and anticipation cartwheeling down Ashley's spine.

'Great!' William said, his eyes lighting up as he saw an advantage. 'Can we go to Springfield Manor with Mr. Cliffton, please, Mum? All you have to do is say you want to,' he pressed eagerly.

Shock froze all the tingling warmth Harry had ignited. He had got to her son behind her back before she could extract a promise from him not to mention Springfield Manor to William. It was playing dirty, getting William on side against her.

She turned to her son, who was propped on a stool at the end of the counter. He had inherited the blue eyes, the athletic build and the ability to play any sport well from his father, but he had her fair hair and basically her sense of fair play. He never cheated on his deals with his friends, and the fact that he had so many of them testified to the imaginative fun he supplied. She liked her son the way he was. She did not want him reclaimed by the Harcourt family and instilled with values that were not her own.

'Why do you want to go to Springfield Manor, William?' she asked, needing to elicit how far Harry had gone in pursuing his quest and how much he had told William.

'So I can go ghost hunting with Mr. Cliffton,' he answered excitedly. 'I'll be the only boy in the street who has seen a real ghost.'

Ashley felt a deep stab of relief. William still had no idea he was the heir and expected to live at Springfield Manor. No doubt he was already planning how much he would charge the boys to hear a description of a real ghost, and Olivia Stanton would be on the telephone to voice another complaint.

Ashley looked dubiously at Harry. Had he decided an indirect approach through William was his best route to success? 'Are there really ghosts at Springfield Manor? Tell me the truth, Harry.'

'Many,' he replied serenely. 'It was at Springfield Manor that the great bard got the idea for the ghost of Hamlet's father, and Charles Dickens got his inspiration for the Spirit of Christmas Past, the Spirit of Christmas Present and the Spirit of Christmas Future.'

'This has to be fabrication,' Ashley observed sceptically.

His eyebrows lifted in a display of innocence. 'Would I fabricate to you?'

'Probably. To get your own way.'

He looked pained. 'Not at all. You must remember that the winter nights at Springfield Manor are very long and very cold. We spend a great portion of these hours sitting around the fire telling stories.'

William looked fascinated.

Ashley didn't know what to believe. Harry rolled out these stories as though imbued with them, yet she had witnessed how quick he was with clever and manipulative responses to Gordon Payne and Olivia Stanton.

'Don't you have TV at Springfield Manor?' she asked, determined on emphasising the present day instead of the long, historical past.

'There are many sets, but rarely used. Not only are our own stories more lively and less boring than those on the television, it is our belief that families that talk together, stay together.'

Solid principles there, Ashley thought. If true.

Harry sounded so good, looked so good, but was it all a masterly performance to get his own way? Ashley reminded herself he had openly admitted he was a man who would not accept no for an answer. It was as well to keep remembering that. How was she to know if his interest in her as a woman was not merely a ruse to charm, even seduce her into doing what he wanted? Did he consider a widow fair game?

William was already putty in his hands. He had done everything right there, aiding and abetting

William in his schemes, filling his head with intriguing myths about Springfield Manor, appealing to the boy in ways that would plant her son firmly at his side in a battle about the future.

'Is this your first trip to Australia, Harry?' she asked, her eyes challenging the twinkling confidence in his.

'Yes, it is.'

'Then may I suggest it's an opportunity for you to learn about a wider range of life than what is incorporated in Springfield Manor. Perhaps you could try to forget that small part of England for the rest of this evening.'

'Aw, Mum,' William protested, 'we were in the middle of a story about—'

'It can keep to another day, William,' Harry inserted smoothly. 'It will hardly be a jolly evening if we bore your mother.' He smiled at Ashley. 'I would love to hear all about your life here.'

He sounded genuine. He looked genuine. He had accepted her block on Springfield Manor with good grace. The rest of the evening should go her way, Ashley thought with satisfaction. Given that he intended to stayed until he succeeded in his mission, she would have plenty of time to find out whether Harry's attraction to her was genuine or not.

CHAPTER SIX

HARRY insisted on serving their meal. Ashley insisted on his joining them at the table. It improved William's table manners no end, and the ham salad followed by ice-cream and freshly cut strawberry mangoes never tasted better.

It was a marvellous evening. Ashley didn't have to do a thing except enjoy Harry's company. In between delving into all the important events of her life as though he was fascinated by everything that had contributed to the person she was now, he cleared the table, whizzed the plates into the dishwasher, cleaned up the kitchen, made and served coffee, saw William off to bed and generally performed all the duties of a housekeeper and parent while making Ashley feel special and extraordinary.

She had never been so pampered, never been the focus of such concentrated attention, never been so appreciated, never had her needs catered to with such charm and finesse. Certainly Roger had never done that. Harry had to be very close to the perfect man, she decided, feeling as intoxicated as though she had drunk a bottle of champagne.

William had not been ignored, either. Harry had generously committed himself to taking him to the Sydney Cricket Ground to watch a day of the test match between England and Australia, since cricket was William's abiding passion at the moment. That was only if Ashley could spare him for a day, which of course she could, for her son's pleasure.

The more Harry committed himself to staying with her and William, the more chance she had of really getting to know him. Ashley had the feeling she could be very happy with Harry Cliffton. He was a giver, a listener, a man who didn't have to prove himself a superior being by reducing women to nothing. Everything he had demonstrated so far put him on a completely different plane to Roger.

Could he be weaned away from his life at Springfield Manor? *As long as it takes*, Ashley thought, deeply pleased that she had a considerable amount of time on her side before any decisions had to be made.

She wandered out to the back veranda while Harry saw William to bed. It was a beautiful balmy night, the sky littered with bright stars, a three-quarter moon beaming enough soft light to take away the darkness, a gentle breeze wafting cooler air in from the sea. The house was only a few kilometres from the beach, and Ashley fancied she could hear the distant sound of surf breaking on the sand.

It was a night made for romance, and Ashley felt her body quivering with the need for it. So many years had been barren of any romance since Roger. She hadn't trusted it, hadn't wanted to invite more disillusionment, hadn't met anybody who attracted her enough to give it a chance.

Would Harry answer that need, she wondered? Would he succumb to more than a professional involvement with her?

The glass door to the family room slid open. 'Can I get you anything, Ashley? An iced drink?'

The caring tone in Harry's voice made her pulse quicken. She flashed him a smile. 'No, thank you. I was just having a breath of fresh air before going to bed.'

'Mind if I join you?'

'Please do.'

He had taken off his waistcoat and tie. His white shirt, unbuttoned at the neck, shone starkly in the moonlight as he stepped out and quietly closed the door behind him. He moved over to the veranda railing beside Ashley and looked at the brilliant sky.

'Where's the Southern Cross?'

Still concentrating on all things Australian, Ashley thought with a twinge of uncertainty. Was he simply being obliging, the ultimate professionalism of a butler? She didn't want duty from him now. She wanted the man, not the man with a mission. She wanted truth, spontaneity of feeling and confirmation that he felt the same attraction she did.

'There it is,' she said huskily, pointing the constellation out to him, willing him to move closer to her.

'So that's what Captain Cook steered by,' he murmured, maintaining a proper distance. 'It's very distinctive.'

'The Polynesian and Portuguese and French navigators also used it, long before Cook,' she informed him dryly, wishing he wasn't quite so focused on English history. She remembered the Harcourt family line he had shown her earlier, tracing it through to William. A spurt of resentment made her ask, 'Why did Roger's great-grandfather leave England to come to Australia if everything's so marvellous at Springfield Manor?'

Harry gave her one of his quirky smiles. 'He disgraced the family with the dishonourable act of publicly revealing he cuckolded a duke.'

'And, of course, the British considered Australia the dumping ground for undesirables.'

His eyes caught hers, searing away their mockery with intense seriousness as he quietly answered, 'It also provided the opportunity to start a new life.'

Was he making a personal statement or simply soothing any ruffled feelings she might have over her country's convict and colonial past?

'That's been true for many people,' she warmly agreed. Although there were some who clung to an old heritage, looking back instead of embracing what a new country offered. Like Roger's mother. 'William is fifth-generation Australian, Harry. I'm seventh generation,' she added, wanting to impress on him that they were well-rooted here.

He smiled. 'What I've admired about the Australians I've met is their attitude of anything being possible for them.'

'Have you ever thought that other things were possible for you?'

'I'm beginning to.'

Hope leapt through her heart. 'Promise me you won't tell William he's the heir to Springfield Manor.'

'I had no intention of doing so.'

'Circumstances can change.'

'Yes, they can,' he agreed without the slightest hesitation, giving Ashley's hope a further boost. 'Though I must say William is a fine lad, Ashley. A credit to you.'

'Thank you.' She smiled on a glorious lilt of optimism. 'He likes you, too.'

His gaze dropped to her mouth. Ashley's skin prickled, reacting to the sudden tension charging the air between them. *He wants to kiss me,* she thought exultantly. But he didn't move. There was a quality about his stillness that screamed of iron-willed restraint. Duty and discipline stamping on desire, denying it free rein, Ashley surmised, and that in itself was exciting, feeling the tug of war taking place inside him.

She sensed the gathering of purpose. His gaze flicked to hers, and there was certainly nothing impersonal in the dark blue intensity of his eyes. She had the uncomfortable feeling that he wanted to scour her soul. Even before he spoke, she felt herself tensing defensively, knowing instinctively that he had moved beyond physical attraction to a far deeper need.

'What went wrong with Roger, Ashley?'

The shock of the question set her mind spinning. How did he know? She had never spoken of the crushing nature of her marriage. Even at the time, pride had insisted she maintain the public appearance of being happy with Roger. She had not confided her problems to her parents, let alone anyone else. She had hidden the guilty relief she had felt when Roger and his mother had died, accepted the condolences given, and closed the door on a hard-learnt experience that she never wanted repeated.

'Why should you think anything went wrong?' she countered, unaware of the guarded tone in her voice, the retreat from openness in her eyes.

'What people don't say is often more revealing than what they do say,' he answered quietly. 'You've told me a lot about your life. Roger Harcourt was your husband and William's father, yet you did not once refer to him.'

'Roger died seven years ago,' she stated flatly. 'I've spent far more of my adult life without him than with him.'

'Happy times usually engender fond reminiscences.' He shrugged and offered an apologetic smile. 'I didn't mean to intrude. If it's a sensitive subject . . . Perhaps you miss him so much it's still too painful to recall.'

'No. I don't miss him,' Ashley confessed bluntly, recoiling from the idea of letting Harry think she was nursing a long grief that had never been assuaged. 'If he was still alive, we'd be divorced.'

'Why?'

'I guess I stopped hero-worshipping him. I was only nineteen when we married.' Her eyes flashed with irony. 'A pity you didn't come looking for an heir then, Harry. Roger would have leapt at being lord of the manor.'

'He acted that way with you?'

'It had its attractive side for a while,' she acknowledged. 'I didn't realise I was supposed to become totally subservient to another person's will.'

'Do you fear that would be expected of you if you came to England?'

'I don't fear it because I wouldn't accept it.'

'It isn't the situation anyway,' he assured her.

'Well, I guess you'd know,' she said lightly, aware that any other judgement by her would be blind prejudice.

'Yes, I do. I'm sorry you had that experience with Roger, Ashley. I hope you don't judge all men by it.'

'If I did, you wouldn't be staying here.'

As soon as she spoke the words, they seemed to hang in the air between them, gathering nuances, laying bare the fact that she thought him special as a man and that being her butler was completely irrelevant. Still he didn't move, and Ashley felt heat creeping up her neck as she recalled the sad way he had spoken of the woman he had loved. Did the memory of her remain in his heart, keeping it closed to any other woman?

She turned away and stared blankly at the night sky, fiercely arguing to herself that Harry had brought up Roger, so it had to be acceptable for her to ask questions that were just as personal.

'What was her name ... the woman you spoke of, Harry?'

The ensuing silence shrieked of dredging into deeply private areas. Was it too sensitive a subject? Did he miss her so much it was too painful to recall? They were the words he had used in referring to Roger.

'Pen,' he said at last. 'Penelope.' He gave the longer version of her name a soft, lilting cadence that filled Ashley with envy. It left no doubt in her mind that Pen had been very precious to him.

'How long is it since ...' She hesitated, not wanting to sound crassly insensitive to his feelings. 'Since she was with you?'

'Pen died of leukaemia three years ago,' he stated flatly.

Ashley closed her eyes. How awful! Bad enough for death to come suddenly. A long terminal illness had to be grief from start to finish. And afterwards ... who could possibly forget it?

'That must have been very harrowing,' she said softly, her natural sympathy overriding her own interests. 'I'm sorry it happened. To both of you.'

He didn't answer. Ashley was acutely aware she had driven his mind into the past. She could feel a great distance between them that had nothing to do with physical space. She waited, although part of her wanted to tear herself away and leave him to his memories. In some strange way, staying with him was like holding a vigil, paying respect to the dead.

'It wasn't like that.'

Ashley barely caught the murmured words.

'After the initial shock of the diagnosis, Pen refused to allow the situation to become harrowing,' he went on quietly. 'She made each day a celebration of life, finding joy and beauty and pleasure in even the smallest things. There were times when the treatment made her very sick, but she bore it so gallantly....' He shook his head. 'I took it harder than she did. I hated feeling helpless.'

'I'm sure you helped all you could, Harry.'

It wasn't a platitude. Ashley was certain he would have been a tower of strength, supportive, caring, considerate, willing to do anything to make life as easy and pleasant as he could for her. Yet as much as he might have tried to hold death at bay, it was always going to overtake his efforts. She understood his feelings of helplessness.

'I guess her going must have left a terrible hole in your life.'

'She was an adornment to the human race,' he said softly.

How on earth was she going to compete with that? Ashley thought despondently. 'Then you were lucky to have known her,' she said with a burst of envy. 'Not everyone gets the chance to love and be loved by someone so special. Even if it was only for a short time, at least you've experienced it.'

It jolted him out of his reverie. His head turned sharply towards her. Ashley lifted her gaze to his and gave him a full blast of truth. 'Your Pen made part of your life beautiful, Harry. Maybe that makes the loss hard to bear, but you don't carry the sense of having missed out on the best, the sense of an emptiness that has never been answered.'

'Ashley...' His hand swung out, ready to touch. There was something in his eyes ... pity? Anguish? She instinctively backed away.

'I think I'll go to bed. I feel cooler now. Good night, Harry. And thank you for making it such a wonderful evening,' she prattled, carefully skirting any contact with him as she moved to the sliding door.

Somehow he got there ahead of her and pulled the door open. She stepped into the family room, giving him a nod of thanks. He followed closely on her heels. The door clicked shut. Ashley crossed quickly to the staircase. Her eyes blurred with tears as she remembered the bubbling light-heartedness with which she had started the evening. It wasn't fair, she cried to herself. What hope did she have against a ghost who represented perfection?

She hurried up the stairs, hoping he would stay behind and let her escape to the privacy of the bedroom before he followed to his room. She felt him watching her, but at least his footsteps stopped on the floor below.

'Good night, Ashley.' His voice softly floated after her.

She didn't pause or turn. She had already said good night. Tomorrow was another day, she told herself, brushing the tears from her lashes. And she did have something over a ghost. She was alive. She was warm flesh and blood. And Harry found the arrangement attractive. She wasn't mistaken about that!

CHAPTER SEVEN

WILLIAM was up early the next morning. Like most young boys, William had an inquiring mind. Since Mr. Cliffton's bedroom adjoined his, it was a simple matter to make enough noise to wake up the new acquisition to the household without disturbing his mother. He figured he could worm more out of Mr. Cliffton if he had him to himself. His mother had a habit of gliding over grown-up matters. William wanted the facts.

Harry woke before his watch alarm went off. It suited him to be up early. Last night he had inadvertently ended up stirring feelings that had driven Ashley away from him. That had not been his intention, although he didn't regret their conversation.

Ashley's directness had somehow acted as a catharsis for him. She had drawn a perspective he hadn't considered before, and she was right. He *was* lucky to have had Pen in his life. The question now was whether he could or should attempt to make Ashley feel lucky to have him in her life.

On sheer impulse he had embarked on a light-hearted game that had promised to be an amusing challenge, a titillating battle of wits and wills with the added interest of considerable sexual attraction. As George had observed, he had been skating along on the surface of life, not caring if the ice beneath his feet broke. Ashley jolted him into the realisation that he was playing with deep waters.

It behove him to tread very carefully with Ashley Harcourt's feelings. Roger had not been good for her. Harry did not want to inflict any more hurt and disillusionment. He liked her. Very much. She had guts and a firmer grip on self-direction than most of the people he knew. It was wrong to play with the life she had made for herself, yet Harry didn't want to deal himself out of Ashley Harcourt's life at this point.

Nevertheless, he was in two minds about the deception he had so frivolously entered into. He pondered whether he should state his real position as he washed and dressed. He heard William go downstairs and followed him, intent on subtly pumping the boy about the more personal side of Ashley's life.

'Good morning, William,' he started, smiling at the huge bowl of breakfast cereal the boy had helped himself to. 'When does your mother usually wake?'

'Morning, Mr. Cliffton. Mum sets the alarm for seven,' he promptly answered.

Harry had twenty minutes up his sleeve. 'Does she have tea or coffee first thing in the morning?'

'Coffee.' William put his spoon down, deciding to tackle the important question without any beating around the bush. 'Are you going to be my uncle?'

'That's a fairly close blood relation, William. I don't qualify.'

'I don't mean that kind of uncle. I know I haven't got any of those, unless you count step-uncles. Mum's parents got divorced and married other people with kids who are now mostly grown up but we hardly ever see them. And my dad was an only child. I'm not talking about *real* uncles.'

William looked at Harry meaningfully as though he should know the correct import of his question now. Harry didn't care for the flavour of it at all. He found himself recoiling from the idea of joining a queue of live-in relationships that had failed to meet Ashley's needs, then pulled himself up for making unfounded assumptions.

Ashley hadn't struck him as a woman who would lightly invite men into her life. But she *had* struck him as a woman who would kick out anyone who tried to take over.

'Precisely what kind of uncles are you talking about, William?' he asked, seeking clarification before making any judgements.

William sighed, suspecting an evasion. He spelled it out so there could be no misunderstanding. 'Some of the kids at school don't have their dads living with them. Other men move into their houses and live with their mums. Mostly they call them uncle. Rodney Bixell's had three different uncles. He's scored pretty well out of it, too. He got a go-cart from the first, a trampoline from the second and a bike from the third.'

Rodney clearly knew how to play every angle.

'Mum won't let me have a bike until I'm ten because we live on this hill and she reckons it's dangerous,' William continued with obvious exasperation at his mother's judgement on this sore point. There was hope and devious calculation in his eyes as he added, 'Maybe you could talk her into it, Mr. Cliffton. You look as if you could talk Mum into anything.'

Harry had his doubts about that but he hoped it was true. 'Have you had any uncles?' he asked, wanting this point settled unequivocally.

'Nah. No luck yet. That's why I haven't got a bike. Mum's never even gone out with any guys. So I figure since she let you move in, Mr. Cliffton, it has to mean something.'

'No guys at all, huh?'

William wrinkled his nose. 'She only has boring old girlfriends who don't give you anything.'

Ashley was clearly not into sampling whatever was available. Such complete abstinence was, however, a measure of how gun-shy she was of men in general. Which made her acceptance of him highly intriguing. And flattering. It also loaded Harry with a heavy sense of responsibility. He didn't think Ashley would appreciate the concept of having fun, especially if carried into intimate realms while she was still misled as to who and what he was.

'You're a big improvement, Mr. Cliffton,' William assured him, giving him an encouraging grin. 'None of Mum's girlfriends would think of taking me to a test cricket match.'

'Well, I do happen to like cricket myself,' Harry remarked dryly feeling more of a fraud by the minute. George had already fixed a private box for him in the Brewongle Grandstand at the Sydney Cricket Ground.

'That was a great catch you made yesterday,' William said admiringly. 'It saved a window and a bit of Mum's wrath. She wouldn't have stood back and thought what a fantastic hook shot it had been. She wouldn't have thought of anything else but the broken window.' He paused to let Harry appreciate the different patterns of the male and female mind, then pointedly added, 'I wouldn't mind at all having you as an uncle.'

Was Ashley considering the same possibility? Or did being a butler put him in a different category, someone safe, leaving her in control of what did or didn't happen between them? Would she instantly show him the door if he confessed the truth? He had a strong suspicion she would, despite the attraction he was sure they shared.

'Thank you, William, but I'm here as a butler, not an uncle,' Harry said firmly. 'I think your mother would be very upset if you referred to me as an uncle. It would give people the wrong idea.'

'Oh!' William's face fell. He reconsidered the situation and presented another argument. 'But you are going to stay here for a while. I mean there's the cricket and Mrs. Stanton's party and it would be real good if you took my side on a few things. Like you did yesterday about the photos. Mum gets a bit fussy. Not like Mrs. Stanton. But, you know...she worries about small things that are really okay.'

Harry smiled his understanding. 'Good parents are like that, William. You're very lucky to have a mother who cares so much about your well-being.'

'It can be overdone,' William muttered.

Harry cocked a reproving eyebrow. 'William, I have a lot of respect for your mother. She's achieved a great deal by herself. It couldn't have been easy being a young widow with a young child to take care of.'

'She had me to help.'

'Of course.' Harry smothered a smile. 'That slipped my mind for a moment.'

'But she could do with a lot more help. It would be a good idea if you stayed as long as possible,' William pressed, obviously seeing many advantages to himself in having Harry at hand. 'I'd like to get my soldiers painted and have a few regiments ready to move by next week. Otherwise I can't pretend to be Napoleon.'

'Wouldn't you rather be the Duke of Wellington?' Harry couldn't imagine William wanting to lead the losing side in any war game.

There was a gleam of pure animal cunning in William's blue eyes as he answered, 'I thought you'd rather play Wellington, Mr. Cliffton, being English and all that.'

William was clearly a master at holding out carrots. Harry was quite a dab hand at it himself.

'Whether I stay or not will be your mother's decision, William. Right now I'm going to make her coffee and take it up to her.' Harry winked conspiratorially. 'Show her what a good butler I am.'

The boy laughed his delight in their mutual understanding. 'That's how I get into favour. Especially when I want something a bit tricky.'

Tricky was definitely the word, Harry thought as he set a tray for the coffee. As William had pointed out, he was already involved here to the extent of taking him to the cricket match and transporting Ashley in the Rolls to Olivia Stanton's party. Letting either of them down after giving his word went against Harry's grain.

He had to maintain the role he had cast himself in until a decision about the future was made, either by Ashley or himself. Confession might be good for the soul, but Harry had little doubt that he would be banished from the household before he could blink if he stopped being the butler. That would not serve the purpose of getting George an heir for Springfield Manor, nor the purpose of getting to know Ashley Harcourt better.

The latter purpose was far more on Harry's mind as he carried the coffee tray upstairs. He had picked a red rose from Ashley's garden and laid it beside the coffeepot. The romantic touch appealed to him.

He hoped it would appeal to her, too. It was wrong that so much of her life had been barren of romance.

He heard the clock alarm go off as he approached her bedroom door and waited until it clicked off before knocking.

'Yes?' A drowsy question.

'It's Harry with your coffee,' he answered.

'Oh!' A pause filled with rustling movement. 'Come in.'

Harry fixed a bright smile of greeting on his face as he opened the door. 'Good morning, Ashley.'

It was just as well he had the words ready to trip off his tongue, because desire hit him in the solar plexus with breathtaking speed, stopping him in his tracks. She was sitting up in bed, a sheet pulled up to cover her breasts but not the two red lace straps that were obviously attached to a very feminine nightie. The pale silk of her hair fell in tangled skeins around the smooth roundness of her bare arms and shoulders. Her face was no less lovely without makeup, and her eyes held a soft, uncertain appeal that pummelled his heart.

Harry knew in that moment it was criminal to deceive this woman in any way whatsoever, yet he was trapped in his own contrived scenario. He didn't want her to reject him. He wanted to take her in his arms, assure her that she was safe with him. He wanted to kiss the slight quiver from her lips, wanted to fill the emptiness inside her with the wonder and pleasure of not missing out on anything. He wanted to give what Pen had given to him.

Perhaps it was another mad impulse, a quixotic urge that could backfire with disastrous consequences. This was not a time for dancing on the edge, he cautioned himself. This was a time for taking things slowly, but his hastily summoned control was severely tested by the sad searching in her beautiful grey eyes. He felt her need and wanted to answer it. Common sense hammered out that it was too soon to know if he could.

Keep it light, Harry, he sternly advised himself, pushing his feet forward again. 'William told me you preferred coffee first thing. Did you sleep well?'

'Yes. Yes, thank you,' she answered distractedly, her cheeks pinking as she turned to clear some space on the bedside table for the tray. 'And you? Were you comfortable enough?'

'Very much so.' He set the tray down and proceeded to pour her coffee. Best to keep his hands busy. It was so tempting to reach out and touch her hair, feel its silkiness sliding between his fingers. Her warm, womanly fragrance was, fortunately, superseded by the aroma of coffee. 'Bacon and eggs and toast for breakfast?' he asked, hoping to put her at ease with him.

'I usually have a bowl of muesli. But please help yourself to whatever you're used to, Harry,' she added quickly.

'It's just as easy to cook for two.' He raised a quizzical eyebrow. She was more composed now.

'Is the muesli a matter of healthy conviction or a symptom of not wanting the bother of cooking and cleaning up afterwards?'

It drew a rueful smile. 'A bit of both.'

'Well, let the bother be mine. I'm here to serve you, Ashley, and I want you to enjoy the pleasure of being served.'

'Then I guess I might as well... once in a lifetime,' she added with a self-mocking twist.

'It needn't be,' he reminded her. 'It could be your lifestyle if you choose to take up residence at Springfield Manor. Everything should be tried... once in a lifetime,' he repeated, feeling somewhat exonerated.

She shrugged. 'What would I do with myself there?' Her eyes flashed derisively. 'In between being waited on hand and foot.'

'Interest yourself in the occupations of others. As you do now. There are estate farms and a village and—'

'I'd be welcome to poke my nose into their business?'

'Helping and interfering are two different things.'

'I'd be an outsider, Harry. A fish out of water.'

'We're all outsiders at one time or another. I'm an outsider here, but that doesn't stop me from getting involved and being helpful and caring. Saying you're an outsider is an excuse for doing nothing.'

'Is it your duty as a butler to hand out homilies with coffee?' she asked dryly as he put down the coffeepot.

He flashed her a smile. 'I'm a man with a mission. You can't expect me not to argue my case.'

'You do it very well.'

His eyes held hers. 'I think you could make a place for yourself anywhere, Ashley. Given the desire to.'

Her gaze didn't waver. 'I think you could, too.'

The zest of contest rippled through Harry again. A defiant pride and a will of steel had overlaid the vulnerability that had so touched him when he had entered her bedroom. The simmering challenge in her eyes put him and his beliefs and his heritage on notice that she was not about to be bowled over by any of them. Anything he won from her would be hard earned. But worthwhile.

Harry's blood stirred. 'You'll join me for bacon and eggs?' he asked, pressing for a crack of compliance.

'I'll dance with you, Harry, but don't assume I'll accompany you home,' she answered.

He grinned. 'Then let's make the dance a merry one.'

His feet were light as he exited from her room. Ashley had accepted the game, come what may, and it was fun again. Apart from which, playing the butler wasn't so deceptive because she would have all that he represented if she came with him in the end.

And more.

CHAPTER EIGHT

ASHLEY pondered her position as she dressed for the day. Harry had reaffirmed his mission, leaving little room for the pipedream that she might be able to keep him in Australia with her. He would go back to England. That was the inevitable reality, and it ill behove her to let it slip from her mind and think other foolish thoughts.

England represented Roger's side of the family. It also represented closer memories of Harry's beloved Penelope. The prospect of taking up residence in Springfield Manor held no attraction for Ashley. Unless Harry overcame all her objections to it.

He had openly declared that he would test her resistance to the limits and he was not inclined to take no for an answer. Ashley wondered how far he would use the tug of attraction to get his own way. He found her desirable. She no longer had any doubt about that.

For several electric moments, when he had first entered her bedroom, she had felt the strong swirl of wanting from him like a physical touch on her skin, a clamp on her heart. He had tried to hide it, tried to ignore it, but it had been still pulsing from him as he poured her coffee. All her senses had been alive to it, treacherously responding to it even as she struggled for the same self-control he imposed upon himself.

But desire wasn't love, Ashley cautioned herself. Desire could be manipulated for purposes that had nothing to do with love. Men and women had been doing that to each other since Adam and Eve. Desire could be a trap that would cost her dear in the end if she succumbed to it. Ashley had been the victim of one man's ego. She didn't intend to ever let that happen again.

Was *winning* uppermost in Harry's mind?

Did he want to be with her as much as she wanted to be with him?

The wise thing to do, Ashley decided, was wait, watch and listen while keeping a good sparring distance from Harry Cliffton. Having settled on this sensible course of action, she headed downstairs for breakfast, confident of holding true to herself despite all the persuasive tactics Harry could come up with.

William was discussing the merits of spin bowling with Harry, swapping reminiscences of the great masters of the art. There was not the slightest hint of being patronising from Harry. They chatted away as equals, and William was very much enjoying the company.

Ashley suddenly felt inadequate as a single parent. It was impossible to be both mother and father to a child, to be the full complementary mixture that answered all needs. Not many people achieved that ideal, she assured herself, dismissing a twinge of guilt at her emotional rejection of her dead husband and her indifference about actively looking for another.

'Hi, Mum!' William greeted her cheerfully. 'I'm going to have bacon and eggs, too.'

Ashley's guilt returned and persisted when the three of them sat down to the cooked breakfast. Like a proper family, she thought, beginning the day together, sharing amiable conversation. Usually William had his cereal and was about his business before she got up in the morning. Her routine was to read the newspaper as she ate her muesli. They only really shared the evening meal, and more times than not the television was on so conversation was mainly limited to ad breaks.

She remembered Harry saying that although there were television sets at Springfield Manor, interesting conversation always took priority over watching programmes. Ashley decided to revise the habits she and William had fallen into. Good communication was important and time should be made for more of it. *Families that talk together, stay together.* Harry was right about that.

'Do you have a busy day ahead of you, Ashley?' he asked.

'Yes.' She explained what had led up to Gordon Payne's visit yesterday and Cheryn Kimball's present predicament. 'Cheryn thought she had a good, secure job and was counting on the income. Given the circumstances, I doubt he'll even pay her what he owes for the week's work. I must try to place her again as quickly as I can. The poor girl was completely distraught yesterday.'

'Can I help you with anything?'

'No. It's kind of you to offer but this is my job and I know how to handle it.'

'You can help me paint my soldiers,' William chimed in, eager to fill in any gap in Harry's time.

'This afternoon,' he agreed. 'Since your mother doesn't need me here, there's a few other things I'd like to do this morning. Reprovision the fridge and pantry, for one. I can't be eating all your mother's food without contributing something.'

'There's no need . . .' she started.

He smiled, melting the protest on her tongue. 'I want to. Let me surprise you. It will give me great pleasure to provide a few special meals for you.'

'The kind of meals you have at Springfield Manor?' she asked sharply.

He tilted an eyebrow. 'Is that forbidden?'

It probably made her a closed-minded bigot if she said it was, yet she resented the subtle pressures Harry was applying to undermine her negative attitude to his mission. She forced a smile. 'Please feel free to provide whatever you like. As I understand it, you take full responsibility for the money you spend on us.'

'You do?' William's eyes lit up like Christmas trees. 'Can I come shopping with you, Mr. Cliffton?'

'You might find it boring, William,' Harry warned.

'Are you going in the Rolls Royce?'

'Yes.'

'Then I won't find it boring.'

'You need your mother's permission.'

'Mum?'

Ashley eyed her son sternly. 'You may go, William, but you are not to ask Mr. Cliffton to buy you anything.'

'I promise I won't ask him,' he agreed quickly. A fair bit of hinting could easily be achieved, William thought, his mind leaping to certain shops that could be artfully included in the itinerary.

Ashley retired to her office once breakfast was over, leaving Harry and William to make whatever arrangements they liked between them. She heard the Rolls Royce arrive and hoped William wouldn't find it too pleasant and addictive. They popped their heads into the office to say goodbye, and the house felt strangely empty when they were gone.

Ashley did her best to settle to work. She carefully scanned the Positions Vacant lists in the local newspaper, mentally matching them against the files of her clients for possibilities to pursue. There was nothing that would really use Cheryn's abilities.

She made several telephone calls, scouting employers who had used her agency to find good employees in the past. One of them had a friend who had mentioned a need for an attractive front-office girl with superior secretarial skills. Ashley wasted no time in making the contact and interesting him in the service she could provide. An appointment was made to discuss the matter further, and Ashley hoped it would result in a suitable position for Cheryn.

A few calls came in asking for temps. Ashley had no problem in filling these requirements. She wondered how Gordon Payne was getting on with finding someone to fit his needs and was glad the responsibility was no longer hers. She couldn't, in all conscience, place anyone in such a demeaning situation.

Her gaze drifted to the Lladro clown that Harry had rescued for her, and the scene replayed itself in her mind, pausing over the sense of connection when their eyes had first met. Had it merely been some spark of chemistry ignited by the tension of the moment, or was it an instinctive recognition of fellow travellers on a plane that was subtly removed from other people?

Ashley realised that since her escape from marriage to Roger, she had been content to hibernate emotionally from all other men. She suspected Harry had done the same after Pen's death, withdrawing himself from any close involvement with other women. Had their meeting snapped them both awake, seeding an awareness of needs they had buried? Were they meant to come together or was this encounter simply a turning point in their lives, a spur to reappraising where they had been and where they would go from here?

The realisation came to her that she had been building a *safe* self-containment. Harry tapped a yearning in her for all she was missing out on. Perhaps it was self-defeating to cling to the control she had achieved. Could what she most wanted be gained without risk? What if she was to go to Springfield Manor with Harry....

She shook her head over such impulsive madness. She had only known the man one short day. It was far too soon to consider throwing up everything on the chance that Harry Cliffton was the man to fill the empty places inside her with the satisfaction she craved.

The buzz of the telephone was a pertinent reminder she should be concentrating on work. She picked up the receiver and crisply identified the agency and herself.

'Ah, Mrs. Harcourt... Gordon Payne here.'

Ashley instantly tensed, expecting his demands and threats to be renewed. 'What can I do for you, Mr. Payne?' she said coolly, determined not to lose her temper this time no matter how provoked she was.

He cleared his throat. 'I was out of line yesterday, Mrs. Harcourt. Said things I didn't mean. I'm a man who's set in my ways and I like things to run smoothly, you know?'

'Perhaps mistakes of judgement were made on both sides,' she offered, astonished at the conciliatory tone and happy to meet it halfway.

'Very upsetting. A bad day all round. I regret my behaviour with you, Mrs. Harcourt, and I hope you'll accept my apology.'

Incredulity billowed through Ashley's mind. Roger had never apologised. Maybe she had over-inflated Gordon Payne's ego and it wasn't quite so monstrous, after all. 'Thank you, Mr. Payne,' she said, struggling to gather her wits and say something gracious. 'I'm sorry we couldn't have reached a better understanding.'

'I'll put two cheques in the mail today. I presume you'll pass Miss Kimball's on to her.'

'Yes, I will. Thank you. She'll appreciate it.'

'I don't want any trouble.'

'Neither do I, Mr. Payne.'

'You'll have no cause to bring any harassment charges against me. I promise you that.'

Ashley's eyebrows shot up. She hadn't even begun to consider such a means of redress. Even if Gordon Payne had carried through on his threats, how on earth could she have proved he was behind the harassment? People like him always covered their tracks.

'I'd be obliged if you'd assure Mr. Cliffton I've put everything he demanded in train and there'll be no reason to get into litigation.'

Harry?

Enlightenment blossomed.

Harry had overheard the threats. He was a witness. He must have gone shopping for a peaceful and fair resolution to the Gordon Payne problem, as well as food to lead her into temptation.

Images of Harry deftly turning Gordon Payne inside out with clever arguments and putting the fear of messy legal action into him flashed through Ashley's mind. She clapped her hand over her mouth to stifle a wild giggle. She wished she'd been there to watch him run rings around the pompous power monger. It must have been a marvellous performance. A Rolls Royce definitely had the weight to buy more lawyers than a Daimler, and undoubtedly Gordon Payne respected that kind of money.

Having sobered herself enough to speak, Ashley blithely said, 'I'll certainly repeat the content of this call to Mr. Cliffton.'

'Thank you, Mrs. Harcourt. I won't trouble you any further. Good day to you.'

Ashley put the receiver down and laughed out loud, joy and relief bubbling through her amusement. She felt like dancing. Harry had done it again! The dragon had been slain by her irrepressible white knight. Was it any wonder that she was in danger of falling in love with him? If he kept on righting the wrongs in her world...

But what if he saw it as simply settling her affairs, smoothing the path for her to wind up her business without any hassles before leaving it behind? That was part of his mission, wasn't it? This act of gallantry might not be inspired by any personal wish for her well-being at all.

On the other hand, she was very grateful for the outcome, so why should she quibble about motives? She snatched up the telephone and dialled Cheryn Kimball's number, delighted that she could pass on some good news and brighten Cheryn's day.

Despite the many question marks in her mind, Ashley could not repress her high spirits when Harry and William arrived home from their shopping trip. She heard the Rolls Royce purr to a halt and hurried out of the office to open the front door for them. Harry and William emerged from the back seat, Harry using his silver-tipped walking cane with elegant panache as he stepped out, his beautiful three-piece suit stamping him as a man of class, William following, happily clutching a bag emblazoned with the toy shop logo.

Ashley moved out to the porch, eyeing her son with exasperation. 'William, I told you....'

'I didn't ask, Mum,' he expostulated. 'Mr. Cliffton said we couldn't have a proper war game without model cannons and cavalry. It was his idea. I just showed him where they could be bought.'

'Led him there by the hand, did you?'

'Aw, come on, Mum. Mr. Cliffton doesn't need leading. He's the smartest man I know.' William broke into a run. 'I'll duck upstairs and put these away. Then I can help the chauffeur with the other shopping bags.'

Such virtue was highly suspicious, but Ashley let it pass. She looked at the smartest man William knew and was inclined to agree with her son.

Harry's mouth was twitching with amusement as William bolted past his mother. His blue eyes danced with mischief.

'I don't suppose you'd know anything about the cavalry arriving in Gordon Payne's office this morning,' she said archly. 'I got the impression that a few cannons were fired there, as well.'

'I love cavalry charges. Did you know in the Battle of—'

'Let me guess. One of your ancestors led it.'

'No. He blew the bugle.'

'As you did with Gordon Payne.'

He grinned. 'It seemed like a good tune to play.'

Ashley couldn't help laughing. 'It worked. The enemy has been routed, and the money is in the mail.'

'A celebratory lunch is in order?'

'It certainly is. And thank you, Harry, both for Cheryn and myself. You're a great bugle player.'

He laughed, and a sweet harmony danced between them, dispelling the defensive reservations Ashley had meant to hold. Harry was a prince amongst men, and there was simply no sense in dimming the pleasure he brought into her life.

They had a positively sinful lunch. Moet and Chandon champagne, cold lobster and an array of exotic salads, plus a selection of temptations from a French patisserie. William made short work of a large slice of chocolate mud cake. Ashley succumbed to an exquisite mille-fleur. Harry produced everything with irresistible flair, and it would have been absurdly churlish to stand on some independent dignity in the face of such treats.

Last but not least, he presented Ashley with a box of Belgian chocolates. 'To help pass the time sweetly in your office this afternoon,' he said with a smile that would have charmed the stoniest heart.

By this time, Ashley's heart was well and truly under siege. She retreated to the safe confines of her office, which was the sensible thing to do, but she couldn't rid herself of the feeling it was a stupid waste of time. How long would she have Harry in her life?

She found it impossible to settle to any productive work. Her mind kept wandering to what she could be doing with Harry—lazing the afternoon away on the beach, showing him some of the scenic beauty spots on the central coast, revelling in his sparkling company.

She wondered how he would look stripped down to a brief pair of swimming trunks. It occurred to her that his skin should be very pale, particularly since he had come from an English winter, yet it wasn't. Where had he got the light golden tan that gave his face and hands such a warm glow of vitality?

Perhaps he accompanied the master of Springfield Manor to the Caribbean to escape the cold. Ashley could well imagine Harry arranging vacations he would find attractive. She suspected he organized quite a lot to suit himself, then used his persuasive powers to make others feel pleased he had gone to so much trouble for them.

A clever manipulator. She mustn't forget that. Underneath all the charm, there burned a steady, relentless and ruthless purpose. He would wear her resistance down until she surrendered to his will. But what precisely was his will? Simply to get William to Springfield Manor for his master? Or did he have some personal desire to have her there for himself?

The doorbell rang.

As she rose from her desk she heard Harry and William come into the hallway from the kitchen. It was a butler's job to answer doorbells, Ashley reminded herself, but she was drawn to the office door to see who was calling anyway.

It was a florist. Harry took receipt of a magnificent bunch of white carnations, thanked the delivery person, shut the door and turned to present them to Ashley as she came forward.

'Wow! Chocolates *and* flowers!' William remarked with unconcealed glee. 'You're doing real good, Mr. Cliffton.'

It drew an ironic smile from Harry. 'They're not from me, William.'

His face fell. He frowned at Ashley as Harry handed her the carnations, two dozen of them prettily set off with sprays of baby's breath. 'Who's giving you flowers, Mum?' he demanded.

Ashley was at a loss to answer until she read the accompanying card. Then she laughed. 'It's a peace

offering from Gordon Payne.' Harry must have
fired a whole salvo of cannons to wring these expensive blooms out of her erstwhile enemy.

William was not amused. 'Who's Gordon
Payne?' he asked in a darkly disapproving tone.

'A gentleman who did some business with me,'
Ashley replied, and took the opportunity to deliver
an appropriate rebuke. 'He was here yesterday
afternoon and but for some very timely inter-
vention, young man, you would have broken the
windscreen of his Daimler.'

'Wish I had,' William muttered.

'I beg your pardon?'

Mutiny looked her in the eye. 'I don't want him
coming around to our house and giving you flowers.
You didn't even tell me about him,' he went on
accusingly.

'I'm not in the habit of discussing my business
with you, William,' Ashley reproved, taken aback
by what was plainly an aggressively rebellious
stance.

'If he's sending you flowers, it is my business,'
he argued. 'I want Mr. Cliffton to be my uncle. I
reckon he'll be tons better than any uncle Rodney
Bixell's ever had.' He marched over to Harry's side.
'So I'm telling you right now, Mum. This is where
I stand.'

Ashley was stunned speechless. She knew children
were growing up rather too fast these days, but to
have her nine-year-old son claiming the right to
choose a live-in lover for her was a bit much to

swallow. Even if he was echoing her own secret fancies.

A flood of embarrassment swept a tide of heat up her neck. She couldn't meet Harry's eyes. What had William been telling him? Or worse, proposing to him? Did he think she was to be had as easily as Rodney Bixell's mother?

Harry, characteristically, took William's declaration in his stride. 'Thank you for your vote, William,' he said with superb aplomb. 'I don't think you need worry about Gordon Payne.'

William looked up, eyes glistening with hope and something suspiciously like hero-worship. 'You mean you'll fight him for Mum?'

'A duel to the death,' he promised, blithely uncaring that William was taking a personal and not a professional slant on this totally misdirecting piece of gallantry.

Ashley found her voice. 'That's enough!' she snapped, her eyes flashing a fury of pride between the two of them. 'I will not have either of you arrange my life for me.'

'It's my life, too,' William pointed out with irrefutable logic.

'Go upstairs this instant, William,' Ashley commanded, losing patience with him. 'I'll talk to you later.'

She thrust the bunch of carnations at Harry. 'You finagled these. You deal with them. And after you've done that, I want to see you in my office.'

Having seized control out of threatening mayhem and impressed her displeasure on both of them, Ashley strode into the private sanctum where she had always ruled the roost. She slammed the door behind her to drive home the fact that she was the boss here. Her own boss. Those who lived under her roof had better toe her line.

Which was all very well, but as Ashley paced around her office in a ferment of passionate conviction about her own autonomy, an insidious little voice in her mind persisted in questioning what her line was. It was utter hypocrisy to deny that her own desires ran parallel to her son's feelings as to Harry's role in their lives. How, in all honesty, could she reprimand her son for virtually giving her the go-ahead to take what she had been dreaming about most of the day?

But Harry shouldn't have encouraged him to believe there was a chance of him becoming his uncle, going so far as to suggest he would fight any other man for the position. It was wrong, without conscience.

Unless he meant it.

CHAPTER NINE

HARRY stepped into the office and closed the door quietly behind him. His demeanour was completely unruffled. To Ashley's intense relief he wasn't smiling. Nor was there any amusement twinkling in his brilliant blue eyes. She was so churned up, any trace of a humourous response from him might have triggered a burst of angry frustration.

She realised, after a few fraught seconds, that the tension in the room wasn't entirely hers. His relaxed air was a cloak, another act of self-discipline. She felt the same sense òf connection she had felt yesterday, stronger now with their knowledge of each other, pulsing with the need to broaden it, deepen it.

Goose flesh shivered over her skin. Her heart skipped to a faster beat. She faced him defensively across the desk, yet there was no defence in objects or space. His eyes held hers with searching intensity, with indomitable determination, and she stared back, caught in a thrall of desire that would not be repressed, despite the doubts that plundered her mind of any peace.

'Why did you do it?' she asked. 'It wasn't fair to involve William with our... with—' She couldn't find appropriate words.

'He is naturally involved,' Harry answered quietly. 'He is not separate from you, Ashley.'

'But you let him think...' She gestured helplessly.

'That I want to be your lover?' he finished for her.

She nodded, her throat too constricted to speak.

'I do,' he said simply. 'Why should I pretend otherwise?'

She struggled with his apparently open honesty. 'Last night—' she forced the words out '—you spoke of your love for Pen.'

'She was a very meaningful part of my life. I will not deny or hide what I felt for her. But as you yourself pointed out to me, Ashley, that's in the past. You and I occupy the present.'

It was precisely the argument she had comforted herself with last night, but she knew there were other considerations—their backgrounds, the countries they inhabited, the lives they lived...so much to separate them, even if these feelings could be trusted.

'What of the future?' she asked, struggling to decipher what was right, whether to seize the moment or give more weight to consequences.

'Who can foretell the future? At this moment I want you. More than any woman I've wanted in years.'

She wanted him, too. More than any man she had ever met. She couldn't deny it. Nor could she hide it from the blue eyes relentlessly boring into hers, revealing their own naked desire, compelling an unmitigated response from her. Yet how could she give it? How, when there were so many uncertainties plaguing her?

She had a responsibility to herself and to William to make the right decisions, the best decisions. How could she recklessly turn a blind eye to consequences and take what she wanted at this moment, for this moment, simply because she wanted it? She was used to weighing everything, wary of inviting any possible disaster. But if she rejected this...

Harry moved, impelled to take the decision from her, sweep aside her painful uncertainty with action. He knew he was behaving recklessly, gambling that it would all turn out right somehow, but he didn't care. He had to do it, had to know, had to feel. He'd been gambling with death for years and come out alive, if one could call it life.

He hadn't realised how dull everything had become until he had met this woman. She had awakened him, and he couldn't let go of this new exhilarating vibrancy, couldn't let her turn him away, as she might if he didn't act. She had the strength of will to do it if she decided against him. Time was his enemy. Every second that passed was his enemy.

He quickened his pace, closing the distance between them with ruthless intent. The blood was pounding through his veins and he knew the thrill, the primitive excitement of the hunter, the warrior going into battle. The bugle call was ringing in his head and nothing was going to stop him. He would take all before him, carry her away on a journey of discovery that he desperately wanted, that she wanted.

Yes, she did. It was burning through her, too, this need to join with him, to explore the sense of being truly alive, uninhibitedly alive, wantonly alive, awareness driven to the ultimate extreme. It was in the wild turbulence widening and darkening her eyes. It was in the faint tremor of her body as she turned to face him, watching him round the desk, coming to force the admission from her, taking the responsibility for it, changing what had been to whatever would be.

The future held no meaning for him. He would deal with it as it came. Only now mattered. And now was what he chose it to be for both of them. That was how it was, and she didn't back away from it. Nor was she passive.

When he took her in his arms, her hands lifted to his chest, not to push him away but to touch him, and even this feather-light touch was like a hammer on his heart. He could feel a tingling heat spurting through his body, and it was imbued with the zestful joy and splendour of life, igniting the lust of the flesh to experience and savour all that bound it to this earth, to this woman who made the world bearable again, who breathed sweet air into his lungs and dazzled his mind with hope, with a promise that it wasn't over for him.

There was more.

He gathered her closer, craving her softness, her femininity, the heart and mind of her, the soul that called to his from the same pit of loneliness he had known, the pit where the ashes of dreams resided in a greyness devoid of the beautiful colours that dreams could paint.

The need to pick up the palette and splash all the bright primary hues around both of them in wild abandonment was upon him, irresistible. Let colour fall where it would. Some of it must stick to them. No more grey. Grey was emptiness, the void waiting for a new creation, and the fever to create was too compelling to forgo.

Her hands slid to his shoulders, around his neck, and her lovely face was lifted to his, the lush curve of her lower lip tremulously inviting his plunder, and in her eyes the kindled blaze of hope, the wish, the want, the need to know, the temptation of the dream of life, to share the depths and the heights and everything in between with one who could...who would.

It was a chance, and she couldn't resist it any more than he could.

He wrapped her more tightly to him. Willingly her soft thighs leaned into the rock steadiness of his, muscles taut with the strength of irreversible need. Her belly pressed over his loins, an enticing cushion of promise for the intimacy within. Her breasts, crested with hard beads of excitement, imprinted themselves on his chest. Her mouth opened under the pressure of his, sweet cavern of sensation, of passion released on a whirlwind of need that swirled from one to the other and fused into a tornado of feeling that swept them up in its tempestuous funnel, away from all worldly things, away from yesterday and tomorrow and the pedantic necessities of getting on with day-to-day life.

Passion feeding on passion, bodies straining to appease the long hunger, hands moving to shed the unbearable barrier of clothes, a totally consuming need to bare all to the desire burning through them, to give all, to take all on the chance that it might prove right, the chance that it would add that precious lustre of true togetherness they both sought, the silver lining beaming from behind the dark clouds, the red-orange-yellow sunburst of golden warmth, the deep calm of blue-green peace.

Their physical surroundings were irrelevant. Behind the desk in Ashley's office they sank to the floor, she pliantly inviting, urgently welcoming, offering the cradle of her womanhood with an utter abandonment of any other care, he needing their mating with an intensity that went beyond all rational thought. *Yes* was the beat of his mind. *Now* was the beat of his body. *Her* was the beat of his heart.

And he plunged himself into the sweet, moist tunnel that would take him to the innermost core of this woman, reaching to the door of her soul, urging it to open with every powerful thrust of himself, wanting to find there the culmination of all he had been blindly searching for since Pen had died.

It came. He felt it begin, the exquisite flowering of ultimate giving to him, the utter yielding of self to the most intimate fusion any two people could achieve, the surrender of every particle of separateness, and it was a wild and exultant intoxicant to him. He moved faster, rushing to meet her climax with his, to share the ecstatic stream of pleasure with her, the essence of life itself mingling, melding, bonding to create the most indescribably beautiful union. He spilled the liquid warmth of his seed into the convulsing heat of her womb, and the blissful perfection of it rippled through them in waves, a wondrous rhythm of togetherness fulfilled and complete.

And they looked at each other, their eyes swimming with the glory of it, their minds dazed that it could be...and was...the possibility, the promise that neither had quite believed in, the chance taken and rewarded, the awareness of its vibrant reality pulsing through them.

She lifted a hand to his cheek, stroking it as though in awe of him or what he'd done with her, and it moved him to kiss her with a surge of tenderness that melted the last of the hard casing that had been around his heart since Pen's death.

'Ashley,' he whispered, and it was a prayer of thanks for being the woman she was, for reaching so far into him that the past had fallen away and he could rejoice in the present because she was here, with him, sharing this moment of revelation, of renewal.

Harry... His name was a throb of sweet exultation in her mind and heart. She couldn't speak it. She felt too much, and his lips were grazing over hers so softly, gently, beautifully, and he was still inside her, filling her with the wonder of all he had made her feel.

What she had known with Roger was a pale thing in comparison, leaving her totally unprepared for such an explosion of exquisite sensation, the sheer billowing glory of it seizing her body, holding it in thrall to the movement of his until that moment ... that moment when she was no longer herself but him, too, an entity that belonged to both of them, yet more than either of the two, like an ecstatic star burst that she imagined must have fired the dawn of creation.

It slid into her dazzled consciousness that she wasn't protected against the act of creation that might well be taking place right now with Harry's seed deep inside her, spilled as wildly and wantonly as she had received it. He hadn't thought of it, and she had abandoned all thought from the moment he had first kissed her, abandoned it to the yearning for all she had missed and craved, beyond bearing the emptiness any longer.

What if a child was born of this coming together?

Strange that she didn't care. Perhaps she would care later when the afterglow dimmed, but she doubted it. To know this at least once in a lifetime was worth any price. It was what a man and woman were made for, and Harry had made it happen for her, giving her this precious gift, a memory to treasure no matter what else happened in her life.

He rolled onto his back, carrying her with him, his arms encircling her, hands soothing away what she suddenly realised was a rough prickle on her skin from the carpet. Not once in her marriage with Roger had they ever made love on a floor. She searched for some tiny shock at such uninhibited behaviour and found none. Her office was strewn with carelessly discarded clothes, and she was in a naked, intimate embrace with a man she had known for only one day, but none of it mattered. Only the feeling mattered.

How long would it last? She snuggled her head below his chin and listened to the steady drumming of his heart, weaving music around it, a melody of happy satisfaction she didn't want to end. Let it beat on, she thought, turning now into forever.

Harry lay in contented languor, his fingers weaving through the long, silken strands of her hair, loosed from its pins in the heat of their passion for each other. His senses were drunk with the feel of her, the taste of her, the sight of her, the scent of her. She was beautiful, her skin like satin, her softness more sensual than velvet, her warmth more comforting than any he had known.

He thought of making love to her more slowly, savouring every moment, every nuance of intimacy, but it was better to wait. It was enough to revel in what they had just shared. There was no need to take it further right now.

He should have asked about protection, but he hadn't known beforehand what he was going to do. If she conceived . . . Harry couldn't stop the smile that spread across his face. A child. His child. An heir for George and Springfield Manor. He almost laughed at the irony of it. So unplanned. Yet if it happened, he would leave no stone unturned to change Ashley's mind about coming to England.

He would enjoy being a father. He enjoyed William, clever little devil that he was. Shock rippled through his mind. They had forgotten William. How long would he wait upstairs before coming to investigate what was going on, before the silence piqued his lively curiosity? If her young son opened the office door, Ashley would be painfully embarrassed, mortified, and she might react badly to the gamble he had taken in pushing for the knowledge they had both wanted.

He sighed, hating to end it, but it was the only sure way to protect what they had shared. He rolled her onto her side so they were facing and gently tucked her tumbled hair behind one delicate ear, giving her time to gather her thoughts as their eyes met in a silent questioning of each other.

Not a trace of regret or hint of recrimination. A brilliant silver shone through the grey of her eyes. He knew it was reflected in his.

He smiled. 'I think we'd better move. You have some talking to do with William.'

'Oh!' She flushed in confusion, horrified at her forgetfulness and what might have ensued from it. She scrambled to her feet in a rush, hunting her clothes in frantic haste.

Harry rose and went to the door, leaning against it to prevent any possible entry. 'There's no cause for panic,' he assured her. 'I'm holding the fort.'

She had already put on her panties and bra, which was a shame because he would have liked to watch her dress more leisurely. She flashed him an anguished look, then all movement was arrested as she stared at his naked physique.

'Do I pass?' he asked, cocking a teasing eyebrow, aware that he was not lacking in any manliness.

She gave a self-conscious laugh. 'I guess you could say you have my seal of approval.'

'You have mine, too.' She had a divine shape, petite but beautifully curved and her bones softly fleshed.

She flushed, her eyes glowing with pleasure. 'I've never been in this kind of situation,' she confessed.

He laughed. 'Neither have I. No style at all. Spontaneous combustion.'

She giggled, a delightfully girlish sound, shy, nervous, yet rippling with elation. 'I don't think either of us gets top marks for control. Which makes us even.'

'I like being even. I could take a lot of it.'

She didn't demur. Harry felt a zing of elation. She was not going to back off. She wanted more, as he did.

She looked thoughtful as she continued dressing. She finished buttoning and zipping and started gathering up her hair, twisting it into a knot on top of her head. The action lifted her lovely breasts, reminding Harry of how they had felt against him. Desire shot through his loins again, and it took considerable willpower to reduce the surge of blood so that its effect wouldn't be blatantly evident.

She finished pinning her hair in place and gave a helpless shrug as her eyes sought his in eloquent appeal. 'I don't know what to tell William. I don't know where I am myself.'

'As long as I stay here we'll be lovers, Ashley.'

'But you still intend to go back to England,' she said flatly.

'Yes. My place is there,' he answered unequivocally. 'It's up to you to choose whether you'll come with me or not.'

'As your lover?' she asked.

He paused to consider, weighing his answer carefully. 'Let's see what develops between us, Ashley. One thing I can say for certain. I don't intend to be William's *uncle*, so please don't use that term in explaining where we are.'

'So you aim to continue here as the butler,' she said dryly.

He hesitated. Was this the moment for truth? If he confessed to who and what he really was, would she turn away from him in disgust at his deception? Perhaps feel hurtfully fooled, even over suc-

cumbing to the desire that had swept them both
into intimacy?

He didn't want to risk bringing any element of
change into that. He wanted to know how much
more could be built on it, whether it would grow
into the magical partnership of souls he craved. He
needed more time with her, just as they were.

'I want to be everything to you. I want your every
need and desire to be answered by me. If it pleases
you to let the established order go on, then so be
it.' He gave her a whimsical smile. 'Being a butler
doesn't preclude me from being your lover until
such time as you decide what you want.'

She slowly nodded. 'We'll need to be discreet.
Especially in front of William.'

'That probably would be best,' he conceded re-
luctantly. 'There's no good in raising his expectations if you know you'll never meet them, Ashley.'

'Me?'

'Yes. You,' he said seriously. 'I won't be an *uncle*
for William. I could be a father.'

She looked stunned. 'You're thinking of
marriage?'

Why was she so surprised? Didn't she know how
special, how rare it was to have what they had just
shared together? Maybe not with her limited
experience.

'Perhaps we could both think about it,' he said
gently. 'I don't even know if you're receptive to
another marriage after Roger. There's much to explore and resolve between us.'

She said nothing. Her eyes were slightly glazed, her thoughts turned inward.

Harry decided to spell out the situation as he knew it would be for him. 'Remember your question . . . what of the future?'

It snapped her attention to him.

'As I see it, there are two futures for us,' he went on. 'What's between us will either end in a beautiful memory . . . or marriage.'

She shuddered.

Harry didn't know what it meant. He waited, watching her closely as she came to a decision, hoping he hadn't pushed too far. But it was the plain truth. It would be one or the other.

He would never move in with a woman he couldn't commit himself to. Such an arrangement offended his sense of honour. Nor would he move in with a woman who couldn't or wouldn't commit herself to him. It smacked of second-rate convenience. He had a need for all there could be in a fully committed partnership.

To his intense relief Ashley's mouth slowly curved into a smile, although there was an ironic tilt to it. 'Well, as my butler, perhaps you could bring me a nightcap after William is asleep tonight.'

Pleasure bubbled into a wide grin. 'How fortunate I bought a dozen bottles of champagne this morning!'

'Always so provident, Harry,' she said, her eyes twinkling warmly as she crossed the office to where he stood sentinel at the door for her. She reached up and kissed him, drawing quickly away to discourage a full embrace. 'Thank you. Until tonight, then.'

She left him with that promise, and Harry was content. Eventually he would winkle out all of Ashley's thoughts and feelings. He had another chance tonight. It was enough.

CHAPTER TEN

WILLIAM was pretending to be engrossed in painting his soldiers when Ashley entered his bedroom. It was clear that he had said his piece and he wasn't going to unsay it. Ashley had met with her wilful son's passive resistance before.

'I take it that you like Mr. Cliffton very much,' she said dryly, settling onto the end of William's bed.

'He catches on real fast. He doesn't treat me like a stupid kid. He doesn't come the heavy adult. And he knows a lot of interesting stuff. Why shouldn't I like him?' came the belligerent reply.

'No reason at all. I'm glad you do. I like him, too.'

William spun around on his chair, eyes bright with eagerness. 'Then why don't you grab him, Mum? He'd buy us all sorts of great things and he's rich enough to take us to some super places. I bet he'd take me to Seaworld and Dreamworld and...'

'William, he doesn't want to stay in Australia,' she broke in, cutting off his starry-eyed dreams. 'He's here for a while. Then he'll go back to being a butler at Springfield Manor in England, and what he's doing for us now, he'll be doing for someone

121

else over there. He's not really rich. The man he works for is rich.'

'Then how come he's got a Rolls Royce and a chauffeur and can buy anything he thinks of?'

'Because that's what his English boss told him to do while he's here. It's like . . . well, a holiday for him.'

William's brow puckered. 'Then why is he being our butler?'

It was too pertinent a question for Ashley to set aside. She took a deep breath as her mind flew through what she could say without revealing the real crux of the matter. William could have the tenacity of a bulldog. If she told him he was in line for an inheritance in England, she wouldn't hear the end of it, and what it might do to his ego did not bear thinking about. She fixed on a discreet line and delivered it.

'Over a hundred years ago, a member of your father's family emigrated to Australia from England. Mr. Cliffton's real boss has been researching his family tree and he found out we were very distantly related to him. He sent Mr. Cliffton to learn more about us. In return for living with us for a while, he's being our butler.'

William chewed over this revelation for some time. 'So the Rolls Royce isn't Mr. Cliffton's,' he finally commented.

'He has the use of it.'

'And the money isn't his?'

'Not as I understand it. No.'

'But he is a lot of fun to have around.'

'Yes.'

He eyed Ashley speculatively. 'He likes you a lot, Mum. He cares about what you want and what will please you. And the way he looks at you . . .'

Ashley could feel her cheeks heating up. Was their desire for each other transparent to her son? Would every look and gesture make a nonsense of discretion? Yet how could she possibly dismiss Harry now? She had to know more. Not to stretch this once-in-a-lifetime experience to its absolute limit would be a negation of the very best life had to offer.

'I bet you could persuade him to stay if you worked at it, Mum,' William said with confident calculation. 'Even if he isn't rich, I'd still like to have him as an uncle.'

Harry's blunt declaration rang in her ears. *I won't be an uncle for William.* Nor for her, either. It would be total commitment—his way—or goodbye and nothing more.

It was all very well for him to make decisions like that. He had had a beautiful relationship with Pen. He couldn't imagine how marriage to Roger made marriage such a fearful step for her.

Why did it have to be marriage or nothing? He hadn't married Pen. At least he hadn't mentioned it. But Pen had been dying. There was a foreseeable end to it, no promise of a future together. No children.

Instinctively she lifted a hand to her stomach. What if she did conceive? Stupid to take risks when the outcome might not be what she wanted. She must do something about that. She had to be sensible.

She caught William's hopeful look and knew she had to dash it. Harry would not be persuaded into being an uncle. He had made that issue decisively black and white. No greys.

'I'm sorry, William. I'm afraid that's impossible. You misunderstood Mr. Cliffton earlier. When he said he'd fight for me, he meant he would protect me from any harm. That's what good butlers do.'

'Oh!' It was a sigh of disappointment. He reconsidered the situation then gave a resigned shrug. 'I guess we'd better make the most of it while we can, Mum, but it's an awful pity it can't last. It would have been good having Mr. Cliffton in the family. He makes it better, doesn't he?'

'Yes. Yes, he does.'

Harry painted brighter colour into their lives, excitement and interest and wonderful surprises. Would it always be like that if they shared his world? Could it last? Or would the shining newness of it wear off? And after it did, would she be left toeing Harry's line, or the line the master of Springfield Manor insisted upon, with submission to others' will expected and taken for granted?

She had sworn never to marry again. But was she condemning herself to half a life? What she had felt with Harry just now... Would it always feel so incredibly special with him, so exalting and... She felt her muscles spasm in an exquisite reminder of the sensations she had experienced.

Harry could make a great father for William. They certainly seemed to have struck up a happy rapport. But the commitment, the complete change of lifestyle would have long-range effects that were incalculable to her at the moment. Would she and William ever achieve a sense of belonging at Springfield Manor, as Harry clearly had? Deeply and irrevocably.

'Do you miss not having a father, William?' she asked, concerned that he was feeling the lack of a man to relate to.

He grimaced. 'Yes and no. It kind of depends.'

'On what?'

'Well, it's like mothers. I wouldn't want one like Mrs. Stanton.' He screwed up his nose to express his opinion of her motherly attributes. 'And some of the kids have got fathers who just yell at them, picking on them because they haven't done this right or that right. I figure I've got it pretty good, really. I mean, as far as mums go, you're definitely the best.'

Ashley couldn't help smiling, even though she knew William wasn't above a little flattery to sweeten her up, thereby slithering out of a deserved scolding.

'Has Mr. Cliffton got that family tree with my father on it?' he suddenly asked.

'Yes. He brought it with him.'

'Can I ask him to show it to me?'

'If you like.' She couldn't deny her son his paternal line. She hoped Harry would keep his promise not to tell William he was the only surviving heir to Springfield Manor.

'Is it okay if I do it now?'

Harry had had ample time to get respectably dressed. She stood up. 'Go ahead. I'm sure you'll find it fascinating with all the stories Mr. Cliffton can tell you.'

'Thanks, Mum.'

He scooted out of the room, his precious soldiers forgotten with the prospect of further dialogue with Harry. Whom he liked enough to have as an uncle even if he wasn't rich.

What kind of husband would Harry make? As a lover he certainly left nothing to be desired.

She left William's bedroom to go to her own, her son's words echoing through her mind. *We'd better make the most of it while we can.*

Ashley intended to do precisely that. Other decisions could wait. As Harry had said, there was much to resolve between them. In the meantime, she would store up beautiful memories.

CHAPTER ELEVEN

THE days slid by, magical summer days. Even more magical nights. Ashley was loath to bring any note of discord into the happiness of simply being with Harry. She asked no questions about his life in England. It was easy to pretend that was something far off when the immediacy of now overflowed with so many pleasures.

In many ways it was like some idealistic dream, too intoxicating to bring her head down from the clouds. Harry brought gaiety and spontaneity into her life. Inhibitions and planning flew out the window. Over and over again she found herself thinking, 'Why not?' and saying yes to whatever he suggested or initiated.

Their family outings were marvellous fun—a lazy afternoon at the beach, an exhilarating morning spent riding the breeze and the waves in a catamaran, a hilarious evening competing at minigolf, then eating monstrous hamburgers with the works. They picnicked by Somersby Falls and dined on fish and chips at Woy Woy wharf, watching the fishermen and the seagulls.

Both Harry and William inveigled her into sharing their interest in the test match cricket, abandoning work for the day, as she did most days except for following through on absolute-must situations like setting up Cheryn Kimball in the new job she had scouted.

They rode to Sydney in the Rolls Royce, and were ensconced in a private box in the Brewongle Grandstand with a wonderful view of the cricket ground. Drinks were readily available at any time, and a scrumptious buffet lunch was served. She enjoyed watching Harry and William enjoying the game, both of them indulgently explaining the finer points of the batting and bowling to her.

But the nights far transcended the less intimate joys of the days. If their initial coming together had lacked style, Harry more than made up for it, imbuing all that followed with romance. They danced by candlelight and feasted on suppers of strawberries and caviar and lychee nuts washed down by French champagne. Ashley learnt the pleasures of sensuality and for the first time revelled in being a woman, desired, loved, adored and cherished by a man who made her feel she was utterly perfect for him.

When it came to the night of Olivia Stanton's party, Ashley didn't want to go, didn't want to waste the time away from Harry. Nevertheless, the agreement had been made, and Harry took it for granted she would keep her word. He arranged for the Rolls Royce to be standing by to take her in the style Olivia expected, and he and William had their war game all set up to play while Ashley was out.

She felt quite flat-spirited as she dressed, although not to be completely outshone by her mode of transport, she made every effort to achieve an elegant appearance. It was also a matter of personal pride to feel at least equal to Olivia Stanton, who liked to queen it over everybody. Perhaps a touch of vanity entered into it, as well, an underlying urge to show the world, at least her little corner of it, she now knew what it was to be a woman.

Ashley didn't have a wardrobe full of party clothes to choose from. Normally she had no need of them. The only appropriate choice was a black crepe wrap dress that she'd bought for a chamber of commerce dinner.

It had a halter neckline, which she dressed up with gold chains. She fiddled with her hair, achieving a smooth dipping loop across her forehead before sweeping the bulk of it into a soft chignon. A few strands were left curling around her ears, to which she attached long dangly earrings in jet and gold. Her T-bar black suede high heels had been an extravagance—she loved shoes—but they lent a touch of true class.

She applied more make-up than usual, darkening and adding definition to her eyelashes with mascara and deepening her lids with a smoky eye shadow. The black dress demanded red lipstick and a touch of blusher on her cheeks. A dusting of powder took the shine off her nose and added a smooth matt finish to her skin.

An examination of her reflection in the full-length mirror assured her she couldn't look any better. She dabbed some Beautiful perfume on her pulse points, picked up the black Oroton evening bag that had been a gift from Roger so long ago, then went downstairs, still feeling at odds about having to mix with other people when she would much rather stay at home.

It was a measure of how deeply Harry had in-filtrated her life. When she had accepted the invitation from Olivia she had felt quite pleased about it. Her social calendar usually ran to lunches with friends she had made through business, or casual barbecues with families who had a child in the same class as William. She was neighbourly and sup-ported community interests, but she wasn't really close to anyone.

It had seemed enough before Harry. She had not been discontent with her life. Being single was a relief after marriage to Roger, and having kept so much to herself for the sake of appearances during the unhappy years with her husband, she had never developed the knack of cultivating bosom friends to whom she might pour out her heart.

She was a good listener, a sympathetic listener, and she thought she was generally liked by others, but no-one really knew her. Not as Harry did. She had told Harry things about herself, thoughts and feelings, she had never told anybody. He had somehow drawn that depth of intimacy from her, and now she wasn't sure if it was good or bad.

It struck home that if she didn't commit herself wholly and solely to him, Harry would leave an enormous hole in her life when he returned to Springfield Manor. In William's, too, she suspected. Perhaps it was time she stopped existing in a wonderful dream and started considering the reality of a future in England. This party tonight might serve to put Harry's influence on her in perspective, bring her feet to the ground.

He and William were in the dining room, their miniature battle lines in place on the table. They were discussing the rules of their war game when she entered, but they broke off their conversation as soon as they saw her.

'Wow, Mum! You're sure dressed up tonight!' William remarked in surprise. 'Is it a special party?'

She shrugged, feeling somewhat self-conscious about her uncharacteristic attempt at glamour. 'I just wanted to look good and feel good.'

'Then you've more than achieved your aim,' Harry said warmly, his eyes agleam with appreciative interest as they skated over her from head to foot and returned to linger on the loosely tied bow at her waist, obviously the key to unwrapping the package. 'Feeling good is important,' he added, his gaze lifting to hers in wickedly innocent inquiry. 'Is there anything I can do to help?'

Her pulse leapt in anticipation of how he would help later tonight. She could feel her body prickling with excitement as she imagined his hands teasing her dress apart, his head bending to...

The telephone rang.

'I'll get it,' William offered, oblivious of the shimmering tension between Harry and his mother. He darted to the kitchen, leaving them together.

'I'm not sure I should let you out of my sight, dressed like that,' Harry murmured, his eyes ablaze with desire.

'Afraid of competition?' she teased, secretly revelling in feeling sexy.

'No. But if the men at Olivia Stanton's party get out of hand, don't hesitate to call in the cavalry.'

She laughed. 'That's never happened to me.'

'Ashley, you're radiating your awareness of your own sexuality. That stirs a man's hormones. All my hormones are rioting over you right now. I have an intense urge to smudge your lipstick and—'

'Mr. Cliffton,' William called excitedly. 'It's for you. Come quick. It's from England.'

'Uh-oh!' Harry grimaced an apology and left her to answer the summons.

Trouble at Springfield Manor? In some trepidation, Ashley followed him into the kitchen, not wanting anything to change now, irresistibly drawn to eavesdrop on his side of the conversation. William handed the receiver to Harry and shamelessly stood by to listen, fascinated by the fact of an international call.

'Cliffton.'

Apparently that was identification enough for the caller. What followed was not exactly enlightening.

'Yes, sir,' Harry said.

After a pause, 'No, sir.'

It had to be his boss at Springfield Manor. Ashley couldn't imagine Harry sirring anyone else. The heat that had been pumping from her heart cooled into a frightening chill. She desperately didn't want any interference to what Harry had started with her and William.

'That would seem improbable at the moment, sir. I have my hands full. Given more time...'

The interruption must have been a very peremptory one because Harry instantly stopped to listen. The reference to time did not bode well.

'I understand, sir.'

A long pause. Ashley felt her whole body tensing with apprehension.

'Arrangements can't be made in a day, sir.'

A brief reply.

'Very well, sir. I'll keep you informed.'

That gave Ashley hope of a longer stay for Harry. However, the ensuing silence was obviously thick with words from the other end of the line. Instructions, orders...

'Thank you, sir. I'll do my best, sir.'

Harry hung up with a heavy sigh and turned to the two expectant faces hanging on his news. He addressed Ashley, a rueful smile accompanying his announcement.

'That was George Fotheringham, the master's voice.'

'What does he want?' she asked anxiously.

'He misses me.'

Who wouldn't miss Harry?

'He says a good butler is irreplaceable.'

He was. Irreplaceable in every sense. Ashley couldn't argue with that.

'Does that mean you can't be our butler any more?' William asked plaintively, and Ashley sensed her son feeling a pit of emptiness opening before him, just as she did.

'He insists that he needs me at the Manor,' Harry stated in a tone that made it an inevitable reality.

Ashley frantically sought a delaying tactic. 'What about your mission?' she pleaded.

'Yes,' William instantly backed her up. 'You haven't learnt nearly enough about us yet, Mr. Cliffton. I haven't told you any of the stuff Mum doesn't know about.'

'William!' Ashley was distracted by the horrors of misbehaviour this confession implied.

'It was for your own good, Mum, so as not to worry you,' he hastily and piously explained.

'As it happens,' Harry drawled, capturing their attention again, 'Mr. Fotheringham has come up with a solution that he hopes will prove satisfactory to both of you.'

'What?' William asked eagerly.

Ashley held her breath. Her eyes clung helplessly to Harry's. Was he about to reveal the truth about William's position?

His smile had a winning appeal. 'That you accompany me to England for a month's visit at Springfield Manor. All expenses paid, of course.'

'You mean we get to fly on a jumbo jet and...' William raved on, delirious with excitement at the prospect of the great adventure being held out to him. 'Every night ghost hunting...'

A month, Ashley thought dazedly. A month of learning what Harry's life was like. She could put up with any amount of condescension and feeling like a fish out of water as long she could be with Harry whenever he was free. And if she could never feel comfortable with the life over there, the option was open for her to return home. It was like a miracle, handing her what she needed but not locking her into an irrevocable position.

'Ashley?' Harry asked quietly.

'You can't say no, Mum,' William expostulated, his eyes as big as saucers and his mind whirling with visions of plenty.

No doubt George Fotheringham would be subjected to her son's entrepreneurial skills for the entire month. And since William was his heir... Was this offer a trap to keep them there? She looked uncertainly at Harry.

It was as though he read her mind. 'You retain all authority where William is concerned, Ashley,' he stated unequivocally.

His word was good enough for her. Harry had never done her any wrong. She trusted him. Implicitly.

'Please, Mum. Please, please, please...'

Her relief and joy broke into a happy smile. 'We'd be delighted to accompany you, Harry.'

'Yippee!' William cried in an ecstasy of anticipation. 'I forgive you for all your other wrongs,
Mum.'

Done, thought Harry, his answering smile
widening to an irrepressible grin. The gamble had
paid off. Of course, he'd loaded the odds on his
side. The timing and execution of the critical telephone call had been perfect, the outcome
reasonably assured with William as dependable an
ally as Harry had ever had. Not that the boy was
aware of it. He was simply a natural at going after
what he wanted with whatever means was available
to him. As Harry was.

Good and faithful George could protest and scold
as much as he liked, but he would carry out Harry's
will. George's sense of service and duty would
always prevail, no matter how disapproving he was
of the scheme in hand. Not that he should be disapproving. After all, if Harry made everything turn
out right, George would have the very result he desired when he had so purposefully reminded Harry
of *his* duty.

It was up to Harry to pursue his chosen course
with vigour. 'Do you have current passports?'

'You bet we do,' William supplied. 'Mum got
them last year when we were booked to go to Fiji,
only I came down with the chicken pox and we
couldn't go. But just about everyone's gone to Fiji.
England will be heaps better.'

William wouldn't have time for much bragging.
Harry moved into step two of his new mission, fo-

cusing his attention on Ashley. 'I'll see to your visas on Monday and book a flight to London for Tuesday if there are seats available.'

'So soon!' She looked stunned.

'Those are my instructions.'

'But what about my business?'

'We'll attend to whatever is necessary. Everything will be looked after.'

He could see she instinctively recoiled from being rushed, her cautious nature wanting to think it all through. That could invite trouble he'd rather avoid.

'You'll be late arriving at Olivia Stanton's party if we don't move now,' he reminded her, stepping forward to usher her to the front door. 'I'll be back shortly, William.'

Ashley felt her mind was split into at least a dozen pieces, zigzagging off in all directions. As she reached the hallway she gathered enough wits to admonish her precocious son. 'You behave yourself, William,' she said sternly. 'And you are *not* to ask for anything. Do you hear me?'

'Loud and clear, Mum. I promise I'll be as good as gold. Cross my heart.' He grinned. 'I wouldn't risk not going to England with Mr. Cliffton.'

And that was the crux of it, Ashley thought wryly as she accompanied Harry to the Rolls Royce. William was getting totally out of hand. He needed a father. But was Harry any different to her son? Everything seemed to be suddenly out of hand. She didn't feel in control of anything any more.

Harry saw her settled in the front passenger seat, wanting her beside him. As he rounded the bonnet to the driver's side he felt the exhilaration of having crossed another critical line. Not only had becoming lovers exceeded all his hopes and expectations, he had successfully put in place the process of moving Ashley to his home ground.

It had niggled at him all week that not once had Ashley questioned him in any practical sense about his life. A woman who was considering him as a husband surely would. It had seemed to him she was satisfied with collecting beautiful memories while Harry had progressed to absolute certainty about what he wanted.

It was possible that she saw a visit to Springfield Manor as a chance to fill a treasure chest of memories, but it was a step towards him, a step towards the future he could give her. Surely she would see that what he offered was entirely different from the life she had suffered with Roger. He couldn't lose now. No way. She wanted him. And they were great together. No doubt about that.

Ashley didn't look at him as he slid into the driver's seat and started the engine. She appeared deep in private thought. Not worrying, he hoped. He drove slowly, considering how best to make his next move.

'Do you always do what Mr. Fotheringham tells you to?' she asked.

It was a tricky question. Harry didn't want to lie to her. Soon, very soon, he would have to lay out the truth, but that was better done in England when she was under his roof. He could more easily counter a negative reaction there. He chose his words with as much care as he had in explaining George's telephone call.

'We tend to come to an agreement, Ashley. I did tell you that George Fotheringham's family and mine have been connected for centuries. Since the Battle of Flodden in 1513. There is a line of respect kept by both sides and an affection and indulgence that comes from long familiarity.'

'A sense of belonging,' she murmured.

'Yes.'

'That must be... comforting.'

'You can share it, too, Ashley. You and William.'

She made no reply to that. She pointed ahead. 'There's the house. The one where people are out on the front balcony.'

The Rolls Royce was definitely on show, Harry thought with a flash of irony, but status symbols were totally irrelevant to what was on his mind. The driveway to the Stantons' double garage had been left clear, and he drove the Rolls into it for Ashley's convenience. He switched off the engine and turned to her, reaching over to take her right hand and hold it.

She looked at him, her eyes mirroring a fearful uncertainty, but she left her hand in his, perhaps needing the comfort of the contact. Without hesitation, Harry gave her one rock-solid certainty to hang onto.

'I want to marry you, Ashley. Will you think about that while you mix with your friends tonight?'

'Harry...' It was a breathless little gasp as though he'd punched the air out of her lungs. Her eyes widened wonderingly.

'Don't answer me now. I just want you to know,' he said with quiet seriousness. To imprint it firmly on her mind, he repeated, 'I want to marry you.'

CHAPTER TWELVE

THE next few moments were a blur to Ashley. The trip to England, Harry's declaration on top of it followed by him playing the chauffeur, stepping out of the car to open her door for her and see her safely onto her feet... It was all happening too quickly for her. Now he was leaving her at this meaningless party to go home and play a war game with her son, and she didn't have wits enough to stop him, to say she didn't want him to go and leave her here alone.

She stood, stupidly speechless, watching him close her door and move to the driver's side, decisive in all his actions. He entered the Rolls, switched on the engine, reversed out of the driveway, and Ashley felt deserted in no-man's-land.

But, of course, she wasn't. People were watching. People were waiting. People who had made up her world before Harry had swept into it. It was probably a good idea to remind herself of what she was leaving behind before she left it to go to England with Harry, before she made decisions that would affect the rest of her life. And William's. She turned and walked up the steps.

'Ashley! You're looking marvellous!'

Olivia Stanton pounced the moment Ashley stepped onto the broad balcony that fronted the house and gave sweeping views of the sea. Her beady, black eyes were avid with curiosity. She was a tall, robust woman, overpowering in her manner. She grabbed Ashley's upper arms and bestowed a cheek-to-cheek greeting as though they were bosom friends.

'And your butler!' she said in Ashley's ear. 'What a prize! So gorgeous, and I'm sure very obliging.'

She'd had a good view of Harry as he'd helped Ashley out of the Rolls. Everyone here had undoubtedly cast an eye over Ashley's highly unusual acquisition. Olivia drew back and gave her a knowing smile.

'I've never seen you so glowing.'

He wants to marry me.

Ashley dragged her mind off the overwhelming thought and found an appropriate response. 'You look quite superb yourself, Olivia.' The flowing tunic and wide-leg pants in accordian pleat were of some expensive silky material, and its brilliant turquoise colour was clearly meant to outshine everyone else. 'That is certainly your colour.'

She laughed, preening. 'I adore bright colours. But, of course, you're still young enough to wear black and men do find it sexy. I daresay having a man like your Cliffton around the house must be quite exciting.'

'He does make a difference,' Ashley replied, letting Olivia interpret that any way she liked, not really caring what anyone thought. Somehow what had happened with Harry had made her feel quite apart from these people, as though they didn't count in her life any more.

He wants to marry me.

Olivia's husband came forward, pressing Ashley to take a glass of his especially concocted New Year punch from the tray he carried. He was a big man who'd been highly successful in real estate. He enjoyed showing off, and the exotic-looking punch with a piece of pineapple and a cherry attached to the rim of the glass had the same attention to detail as everything he did.

'Thank you, Geoff. I hope it doesn't have too much of a kick,' Ashley said, obliging her host.

He laughed merrily. 'What's life without a few kicks? I bet you enjoy riding around in that Rolls.'

'It's very comfortable.'

'A Silver Spirit, isn't it?'

'So William tells me.'

'Enterprising boy, your William,' Geoff Stanton said approvingly. He grinned. 'Must get it from his mother. Enterprising of you to take on a butler of such class, Ashley.'

'It's certainly been interesting.'

He boomed another big laugh, his eyes sweeping over her in male speculation, obviously seeing her in a totally different light than he had previously. Ashley wondered if his hormones were stirred. Did her new knowledge of herself really show, as Harry said, or was Geoff Stanton's imagination running riot?

It didn't matter. What she felt with Harry superseded everything else.

He wants to marry me.

She wanted to say yes, yet she also wanted to find out what lay ahead, what new turning points she might be faced with. It was good that she and William were going to England. She needed to see what life would be like at Springfield Manor.

'Ashley! Over here!'

It was Sonya Bixell, Rodney's mother, calling and beckoning her to join the group of people she had gathered around her at the other end of the balcony. Rodney's third uncle, a very muscular gym instructor, was prominently at her side.

Ashley excused herself from the Stantons' company and made her way to Sonya, smiling at the outré image she always affected. Her hair was dyed a deep burgundy and highlighted with wide blonde streaks. She wore a purple and green outfit and was bedecked with the arty costume jewellery she designed and made herself. Her penchant for taking and discarding lovers was put down to her artistic temperament, and she was such a bright spark, her company was always welcome.

'Darling! I'm a cocktail of admiration and envy.' Sonya waggled her eyebrows as no-one else could. 'What a move up in the world! A butler and a Roller! How did you do it?'

Ashley grinned. 'I didn't really do anything. They simply arrived. And I thought, why not?'

'Why not, indeed? A man like that doesn't happen very often. I'd have snapped him up, too.'

'Come on, Sonya,' the muscle man protested. 'Not in front of me, please.'

'Take heart, dear boy!' She patted his hand. 'I never poach on my friends.'

He gave Ashley a droll smile. 'Handcuff him to you, Ashley.'

'Uh-uh! Bad move,' Sonya advised. 'That would mean she was handcuffed, too. Keep your freedom, Ashley.'

'Not everyone is a free spirit like you, Sonya,' one of the other women said. 'I like being married.'

'Thank you, darling,' her husband purred.

All marriages weren't bad, Ashley thought.

'Well he is the father of your children,' Sonya conceded indulgently. 'Rodney's father left me holding the baby, and that experience was quite enough for me. Having more kids is not on my agenda.' She grinned at Ashley. 'I bet William's enough for you, too.'

She had thought so, but would she really mind if Harry wanted a child . . . children? If she married him.

'That boy of yours is something else,' Sonya went on, 'taking photos of his friends in the Rolls, then selling them at ten dollars a pop. Has he got your butler twisted around his finger?'

'I think Cliffton has his measure,' Ashley said slowly. She had the strong impression Harry was always one step ahead of both of them. Her wayward son wouldn't be able to get away with quite so much if Harry was her husband. From what William had let drop earlier this evening, some closer supervision was called for. What *was* the stuff she didn't know about?

The conversation flowed onto other topics. She half listened to the gay repartee, more observing the people than hearing what they said. Were they happy with their partners? Did economics and family ties keep them together or did they have a very real emotional commitment?

She couldn't go down Sonya's track. Not with Harry. Besides, she didn't have the temperament or inclination for a life of changing partners. All or nothing. Harry was right about that. Until he had swept into her life, *nothing* hadn't seemed so bad. Now... Well, she would make her decision in England.

Her gaze drifted to the huge living room beyond the glass doors that opened to the balcony. It displayed the very latest in modern furnishings, no expense spared, and display was definitely the key word. The Stantons' home was by far the most impressive in the neighbourhood, and Olivia took great pride in the sophisticated decor. Children were not allowed to play indoors, a matter of some disgust to William.

Ashley wondered what Springfield Manor was like. Such an old place was probably full of precious antiques. She hoped the grounds would be large enough to divert William from playing where he shouldn't. Ghost hunting could become a costly sport if he wasn't careful.

She was startled to see Gordon Payne amongst the guests in the living room, then realised it wasn't unlikely for him to be friends with Geoff Stanton. Building project homes and dealing in real estate went hand in hand. With all that had followed from the delivery of his two dozen white carnations, she had forgotten to send him a thank-you note. Much as she still disliked the man, Ashley decided it was diplomatic to acknowledge the gift.

She waited until she caught his eye then moved purposefully towards him. Surprisingly he detached himself from the group around him and moved to meet her, ensuring a private little chat.

'Mrs. Harcourt,' he greeted with dry formality. 'Quite the little show stopper tonight.'

Crass, Ashley thought, but she put on a polite smile. 'I wanted to thank you for the flowers. It was a generous gesture, Mr. Payne.'

He smirked. 'Pure politics, Mrs. Harcourt. That so-called butler of yours went to the minister of local government on your behalf and was creating trouble for me. Obviously I had to find means to protect myself.'

Alarm jangled through Ashley's brain. This odious man had something up his sleeve. 'What have you done now?'

'I have connections in London,' he boasted. 'I had them investigate your so-called butler and find out precisely who and what he is.'

'There's nothing sleazy about Harry Cliffton,' Ashley declared hotly, hating Gordon Payne's snide manner.

'No? Well, let me tell you—'

A loud commotion distracted both of them. Dylan Stanton came pelting into the living room, dripping blood from his nose and mouth and bawling for his mother and father. To Ashley's horror, William was at his heels, blood dripping from a cut over one eye, but totally undeterred by the wound. He grabbed Dylan's T-shirt and rained blows on his shoulders.

'Stand and fight, you snivelling coward!' he yelled.

'Boys! Boys!' Geoff Stanton shouted, plowing towards the fray as guests shrank from it.

'Oh, my God! They're bleeding on my carpet!' Olivia shrieked.

'He broke my nose, Dad,' Dylan cried.

'William!' Ashley gasped.

'I'll break more than that before I'm through with you, you little creep,' William snarled, grabbing his hair and putting a headlock on Dylan with his other arm. 'You take back what you said about my mother or I'll throttle you.'

'It's true!' Dylan croaked, his arms flailing in an effort to fight William off. An elaborate vase of flowers was knocked from a coffee table, crashing in a mess onto the floor.

'Dirty liar!' William muttered fiercely, unabashed by the chaos being wrought around them.

'Stop it, William!' Ashley commanded, pushing forward to try to pull him off the other boy.

'He said bad things about you, Mum. He's gotta take them back.'

'You young ruffian!' Geoff Stanton roared, reaching them first and tearing the two boys apart.

William stumbled, crashing into the coffee table. Glasses of punch went flying onto a white leather couch, the sticky orange liquid splashing over the cushions and dripping onto the floor.

Olivia screeched. 'It's going to stain. They're ruining everything!'

'Someone get towels!' Geoff snapped.

Ashley reached William and helped him up, relieved to see that the cut near his eyebrow was more a slight split that an open gash. He would end up with a black eye, but of the two boys, he had sustained by far the less damage.

'There's not that much blood,' William said, eyeing the carpet judiciously. 'There would have been a lot more,' he declared without regret, 'if I could have held him down a bit longer.'

'Oh, William!' Ashley cried despairingly. 'How could you?'

'I did it because I love you, Mum.' He glared murder at Dylan, who was now cowering behind his father. 'He said you had the hots for Mr. Cliffton. He reckoned being a butler was just a fancy name for being like Rodney Bixell's uncle.'

'It's true!' Dylan jeered from the safety of his father's back.

'It is not. Let me at him, Mum,' William demanded in a fury, struggling to free himself from her hold.

'My mum saw them in a clinch through your living-room window late one night,' Dylan claimed triumphantly.

Ashley's heart sank. Dancing by candlelight. So much for discretion.

'Your mum couldn't see out of a paper bag,' William yelled.

'This is an absolute disgrace!' Olivia cried, seething with outrage at the despoiling of her perfect house. 'Have you no control over your son, Ashley?'

'What was your son doing out at this time, repeating your tattle to William?' Ashley retaliated. While she didn't approve of fighting, her son had stood up for her. Loyalty deserved loyalty.

'He knocked out one of my teeth,' Dylan wailed.

'Yeah, and I've got it right here.' William pulled a bloody tooth out of the back pocket of his shorts and displayed his gruesome trophy with defiant pride. 'It's gonna cost you to get it back, too.'

Ashley went into shock.

Not so Olivia. 'You little savage! You should be sent to a reform school.' She looked around wildly. 'Someone call the police.'

No-one moved. No-one had gone to get towels to clean up the mess, either. No-one wanted to miss one second of this horror show. It was too deliciously fascinating to all the non-participants. Surreptitious glances flashed from neighbour to neighbour as they wondered what quality of moral direction was being given to their children with what was going on about them. Were they all above reproach?

'Now, Olivia, let's not overreact,' Geoff Stanton demurred. 'I'll take Dylan to casualty at Gosford Hospital straight away. We'll see an orthodontist.'

His wife was aquiver with rage. She pointed an accusing finger at William. 'He has assaulted and maimed our son, wrecked our living room—'

'I'll pay for all damages,' a calm voice interposed, and all heads turned towards it.

The crowd from the balcony parted for Harry to step into the limelight. As far as Ashley was concerned, it was a very timely entrance. She needed all the support she could muster. Her white knight had come to her rescue again, and her heart danced a tune of sweet relief.

A buzz went around the guests as Harry surveyed the scene with his usual charismatic panache, unruffled, assuming authority as though it was naturally his, handsome, debonair, a class act that focused every eye on him. He targeted Olivia first.

'Mrs. Stanton, I regret that I was unable to stop this little fracas. The boys were already fighting when I arrived at the Harcourt residence. On seeing me, your son ran off, with William in hot pursuit, both of them racing through the backyards of several houses, climbing over fences which I, with a recently injured leg, had to negotiate with restraint. Neither boy heeded my calls.'

'My son has a broken nose and a smashed mouth. He needed his mother,' Olivia said haughtily. 'He was simply coming home.'

'After he went to *my* home to stir *my* son,' Ashley pointed out, determined that William not be blamed for everything. 'People intent on causing trouble often get more than they bargain for.'

'How true!' Harry agreed, and blithely related one of his stories. 'It reminds me of the time when Cromwell sent his Roundheads to pillage the village near Springfield Manor. One of my ancestors, Richard by name, resented this intrusion upon his peaceful life. He organised an ambush that pillaged the Roundheads, separating them from their weapons, their clothes and their teeth. They were sent back to Cromwell with the message that he'd better find men with more bite.'

Stunned silence.

Harry gave Geoff Stanton a man-to-man smile. 'I'm sure you understand that an offensive act invites retaliation. Quite primitive, of course, but it is in all of us.'

Ashley suddenly realised that Harry was subtly showing his bite. He was not only defending William's action, but prepared to go to battle on her behalf. Her heart fluttered. Harry was a formidable slayer of dragons.

Geoff Stanton was obviously weighing his response to this challenge. He enjoyed showing off but he was not a stupid man.

Olivia exploded. 'How dare you walk in here and patronise us! What kind of butler ethics is this supposed to be? Just taking over as though—'

'He's an imposter, Olivia,' Gordon Payne inserted loudly. 'He is not a butler. He's never been a butler. And he's never likely to become one,' he added derisively, strolling forward to stand by Geoff Stanton and revel in the reaction to his startling disclosure.

'He is so, too,' William rebutted.

'For you, William,' Harry said quietly. His vivid blue eyes burned intensely into Ashley's. 'And for your mother.'

'A con man,' Sonya Bixell breathed. 'Oh, poor Ashley! He looks so good and sounds so good—'

'I knew it!' Olivia crowed. 'Why would a real butler come here? You've been suckered in, Ashley.'

'She has not!' William denied fiercely, flinging his arm protectively around Ashley's waist. 'My mum is the smartest woman in the world. Mr. Cliffton is real good to her. He—'

'Happens to be one of the richest men in England,' Gordon Payne drawled, enjoying the shock value of this new revelation. He warned his friend, 'And that's a lot of muscle, Geoff. To put it in a nutshell—Harold Alistair Cliffton, landed gentry, upper class, owner of an ancestral manor with attached farms and a village.'

It had to be a mistake, Ashley thought numbly. Yet Harold Alistair Cliffton was the name on Harry's passport. How many Harold Alistair Clifftons were there in England? And Harry wasn't denying it. Harry wasn't laughing as though it was nonsense.

'The art gallery in his home is alone worth millions,' Gordon Payne went on. 'Cliffton has carried on the family tradition of being a highly enterprising financier, and his personal fortune is calculated in billions. A bit of a gambler, but his reputation is that of always being one step ahead of the market. They say he has the Midas touch.'

'I never deal in gold,' Harry said dryly.

Ashley could feel the blood draining from her face. It was no mistake. Harry wasn't the butler from Springfield Manor. He was the master. Master of so much her head whirled at the enormity of his possessions. His power.

He turned to her, his eyes blazing with compelling inner conviction. 'In fact the only gold I want is right here. And I will not have it tarnished in any way whatsoever.'

He swung to Olivia. 'Mrs. Stanton, I'd be obliged if you told your gathered guests what you did see that led to the scurrilous allegations you made in front of your son.'

Olivia went red. 'I won't let you bluff me, no matter who you are. You were holding Ashley in an embrace.'

'We were dancing. There is nothing reproachable in that, Mrs. Stanton.' Harry cast a slow, quizzical glance around the room. 'Is there anyone here who wishes to put some other interpretation upon two people enjoying a dance together?'

It was a mildly spoken question, but simmering behind it was a sword, ready to cut off any head that presented itself. Ashley didn't think anyone was in doubt about that. Despite his air of languid elegance Harry emitted a power that was all the more mesmerising for being understated.

Not a word was so much as murmured.

Ashley noticed that Sonya Bixell looked absolutely entranced. She had a preference for the muscular type, and Harry was displaying a new dimension of muscle that clearly fascinated her.

'Perhaps I should mention that if an action lies for defamation, I'm prepared to exchange the names of our legal advisers,' he went on smoothly, turning to Olivia. 'You have nothing more to say, Mrs. Stanton?'

Geoff Stanton forestalled any reply from his wife. 'I don't believe Ashley would do anything to, uh, compromise her, uh, spotless reputation.'

Harry bestowed another smile on him. 'Thank you. Mr. Payne omitted to relay that I also have a reputation for righting wrongs. I wouldn't want that overlooked.'

He paused to let it sink in, then swung to Ashley and held out his hand to her. 'The car is waiting outside. Are you ready to leave now?'

'Yes,' she said huskily.

She put her arm around William's shoulders, hugging him close to her, not only to inhibit any further outbursts or mayhem from her son as they walked across the room to Harry, but also needing to hang onto the one known constant in her life. Whoever Harry was, whatever he was, he was providing the quickest avenue of escape from this dreadful scene, and she was not about to delay that, no matter how confused she felt over his real identity.

He took her hand in his, warm, strong, comforting. 'Good night to you all,' he said pleasantly.

'You'll pay for this,' Olivia shot at him. She had been upstaged and forced to swallow a public reprimand while seeing her son and husband beaten into submission. The humiliation of it all was a dreadful blow to her self-blown authority.

'I would pay anything for Ashley and William, Mrs. Stanton,' Harry replied. 'Do enjoy the rest of your party.'

Even in her fury she recognised that Harry couldn't be touched. She turned her venom on Ashley. 'Don't think I'm going to forget this. You'll pay, too. And this wretched boy of yours.'

Ashley's chin came up in defiant pride. 'Then you'll need a long arm, Olivia. William and I are going to England with Harry.' She paused, then tossed off the perfect exit line. 'He wants to marry me.'

CHAPTER THIRTEEN

THE Rolls was once more parked in the Stantons' driveway. To Ashley's intense relief, they reached it without further incident, Harry seeing her into the front passenger seat while William scrambled into the back. Harry had them on their way home in a matter of seconds.

As soon as the Stantons' house was behind them, William could repress himself no longer. 'Have you really got billions, Mr. Cliffton?' he asked in a tone of awe.

Clearly, the offense he had taken at Dylan's slurs on his mother had been superseded by the vista of a fortune that even his enterprising mind found beyond his imagination. Ashley empathised with his sense of disbelief, but she could not condone such point-blank curiosity about someone else's private affairs.

'William, you mustn't ask personal questions like that. It's bad manners.'

He sighed. 'Sorry, Mr. Cliffton.'

Harry sighed, too. 'Wealth isn't everything, William. It sometimes gets in the way of more important things. Like people seeing you as a person who has the same needs and feelings as themselves. And the same sense of loneliness and isolation.'

It was true, Ashley realised. One never really thought of wealthy people being vulnerable to anything but their own excesses. Yet when Harry had revealed how much Pen had meant to him, how much he missed her, how empty his life had become, Ashley had listened with heartfelt sympathy, never doubting the depth of his feeling.

As though Harry was tuned in on her thoughts, he softly added, 'All the wealth in the world doesn't have the power of commanding life and death in those whom you love.'

Ashley caught her breath at the underlying pain in those sad words. Was Pen truly in the past for him? He had seemed really happy this week, but he hadn't said he loved her. Did he want to marry her because he had found in her and William some kind of panacea for his loneliness?

'Mum and I see you as a person,' William claimed, having digested the sense of Harry's remarks. 'Is that why you pretended to be a butler with us?'

'Partly,' he answered.

He glanced at Ashley. She could feel his eyes raking her profile, feel his concern about what she was thinking, but she wasn't ready to make any comment yet. Not in front of William. She stared steadily ahead, trying to calm the turmoil inside her. There was a lot to deal with.

'Mostly it was to persuade your mother to let me stay with you,' he added quietly.

Even if he had to camp in a tent in her backyard, Ashley remembered. His desire to stay could not be doubted.

'Because you wanted to get to know us?' William inquired further, working through the situation with commendable logic.

'Yes.'

Ashley wondered if she had been hopelessly gullible in swallowing his butler masquerade. She had wanted to believe it because Harry...was Harry. The desire to keep him with her had been very strong.

His reluctance to reveal his wealth and position was understandable. She had been prickly enough about Springfield Manor and the style of life it entailed. How she would have resented his true situation, assuming he had come to lord it over her and William! She would have shown him to the door in a fury of pride and fierce independence. And she would have missed out on all that had followed.

'Mum, is it true that Mr. Cliffton wants to marry you?' William asked, unusually cautious in putting the question.

'He said so,' Ashley replied, feeling wary herself about being too definite on anything to do with Harold Alistair Cliffton.

'Is it true, Mr. Cliffton? You want to marry Mum?'

'Yes, I most certainly do.' Nothing hesitant about that.

There was the audible release of a long breath from the back seat. Then, on a patently hopeful note, came the question, 'Have you said yes, Mum?'

'It's not a decision I want to rush into, William,' Ashley answered curtly. When it came to turning points in one's life, becoming the wife of a billionaire from the English landed gentry was like having the whole world swing on its axis.

'But, Mum, all you have to do is say yes. Just say yes! Please say yes!' William was off the back seat and hanging between the two front ones, urging her consent. 'Please, Mum, it would be so good for us. You wouldn't have to ever work again or worry about how much things cost. And you'd be free to—'

'Please sit down, William!' she said sharply, hating his reference to money.

He ignored her, all pumped up to fight for what he wanted. 'Look how great it's been this week, like being a real family, and you not stuck in the office all day—'

'William, your mother told you to sit down,' Harry cut in with quiet but firm authority. 'I think you've said enough for now.'

For once in William's life, discretion was the better part of valour. He sighed and retreated, although he had made clear which way his vote had been cast. There could be no conflict about William's future, Ashley thought with considerable irony. It was a tribute to the respect Harry had earned from William that the obedient silence from the back seat was maintained until they arrived home.

'Straight upstairs to the bathroom, William,' Ashley ordered as they entered the house. 'That cut needs to be cleaned and attended to.'

'Would you like me to do it, Ashley?' Harry asked.

'I'm used to it,' she said dryly. 'A pot of coffee wouldn't go astray. I'll be down as soon as I've seen William to bed.'

'Bed!' It was a squawk of protest. 'What about our war game?'

'The war games are over for the night,' Ashley declared very firmly.

'But I didn't do anything wrong, Mum. Dylan Stanton deserved what he got.'

'I want some private time with Harry, William.'

'Oh! All right then.'

Apparently he was prepared to keep the peace for what he hoped was the greater good. He didn't even attempt any further persuasion on the marriage question. Like a docile lamb he suffered Ashley's ministrations in the bathroom, standing still as she cleaned away the blood, then applied antiseptic cream and a butterfly closure to the cut. He swallowed two pain-killing tablets, changed into his pyjamas and settled himself in bed without any protest.

The eyelid below the cut was quite puffy and beginning to discolour. Ashley felt a fierce rush of maternal love as she bent to kiss her wounded warrior son good night. He had fought for her against the scuttlebut and gossip amongst her neighbours. She wondered how bad it had been. What wasn't known had probably been invented. She hoped they felt ashamed of themselves.

Perhaps William's fight tonight had put an end to it. If not, Harry's threats of legal redress would certainly have them thinking twice before opening their mouths again. She smiled. Her two protectors, both of them using the power at their disposal on her behalf. While she still felt confused about Harry's motives, she knew her son's were absolutely pure.

She dropped another kiss on his forehead. 'Good night, William.'

'I love you, Mum. I want what's best for you,' he pleaded softly.

'I know.' She gently stroked his hair. 'I love you, too. When we go to England...then we'll know what's best. Go to sleep now.'

She was committed that far. Maybe she was committed all the way. But there were some things she had to find out first, and she needed the truth now, the absolute truth.

Harry was in the kitchen. He poured two cups of coffee and set them on the counter as she came downstairs, waiting until she reached the family room before looking at her. His face was grave, tense. His eyes had the intensity of lasers, searching hers for some hint of what she was feeling.

'Should I start with an apology?' he asked.

Her legs felt like water, but she walked steadily to the kitchen counter and drew out one of the stools to sit facing him. She settled on it and pulled her coffee closer before speaking.

'Are you sorry for anything?' she asked with creditable calm.

'No. I'd do it all again to have what we've shared this week.'

Well, that was ruthlessly honest, Ashley thought. She lifted her gaze to his, determined on knowing all she needed to know. 'What about your stated mission? Is all of that true?'

'Yes. Except I was the one who wanted to meet you. George Fotheringham is my butler at Springfield Manor.'

Ashley took a deep breath. This was a big question. 'Can't you have children, Harry?'

He looked startled, then somewhat bemused. 'I've always assumed I can. There's no reason I know of to think I can't. Why do you think otherwise?'

'Why come for William?'

He gave her a rueful smile. 'Because George was nagging me. Since Pen died I hadn't formed any suitable alliance for the purpose of procreation, and he was disturbed that the family line might come to an end. That would leave his family unprovided for.'

'So we were the means of letting you get on with your life without any further nagging from George.'

He shook his head. 'It was more a case of getting on with my death until I met you, Ashley. That was what was really worrying George. When I broke my leg in a skiing accident, he instigated the search for an heir. He handed me William in an attempt to blackmail me into conducting my life sensibly.'

She had to smile. 'He doesn't know you very well, does he?'

Harry's responding smile was more a wry twist. 'He does, actually. His need for me to do my duty blinded him to the possibility that I might embrace the Australian connection.'

'Then he's not too happy about us.'

'He will be. If you'll marry me, Ashley,' he said seriously, his eyes blazing with his desire for that outcome.

'And have your children?' she asked, wondering if this was the crux of everything.

The challenge, the uncertainty in her eyes made him pause. Very gently he asked, 'Is that the problem? If you can't have any more children, Ashley, please don't think it's an impediment to our marriage. We can have so much together. More than I ever hoped was possible for me. I hope that's true for you, too.'

'Oh, Harry!' She could barely speak over the choking lump in her throat. Tears blurred her vision. The knots in her stomach started unravelling. He wanted to marry her simply for her, for them to have each other. Maybe she wasn't as perfect as Pen had been for him, but she had given him a reason for living. And he was so good to her!

She barely saw him coming before she was swept off the stool and into his embrace, his arms wrapping her tightly to him. 'Ashley, my love,' he murmured tenderly. 'Can't you feel how much I want you?'

My love?

'I can have children, Harry,' she blurted out. 'But you didn't once ask me about protection.'

His chest heaved and fell, his breath feathering her ear. 'I wanted whatever you wanted, and in the end it had to be your choice. Any man who's as much in love with you as I am would want to share his child with you. That's natural and normal.'

'You decided so soon?' she asked incredulously, lifting her head to see his expression.

A whimsical little smile curved his mouth. His eyes softly pleaded for her understanding. 'Ashley, when you've been in a desert, you know when you've struck an oasis. And you don't want to leave it. Ever. You want to drink from it as deeply as possible. But if you don't want another child...'

'I didn't say that,' she quickly demurred. 'I wanted to be sure I would be more to you than the mother of your heirs.'

'The only mother I want for my heirs is a woman I love, Ashley. The loving comes first. And if children are born of that love, well and good. If not, we still have William. I'll adopt him.' He suddenly grinned. 'That boy needs a father.'

She laughed, joy bubbling up to dissipate the last little shadows of doubt. 'Do you think you're up to the challenge?'

'I must confess I could never resist a challenge. Will you take the chance and marry me?'

'I don't know what's expected of a billionaire's wife, let alone—'

'There are only two requirements.'

'What are they?'

'Love me.'

How could she not love him? He gave her everything she had ever dreamed of in a partner for life. 'And the other?' she asked.

'Let me love you. No restrictions. No restraints. Let me shower you with all the love I want to express in all the ways I can think of, because we only live once, Ashley, and we must make the most of every moment while we can.'

'Yes,' she agreed, knowing he was thinking of Pen, but it didn't matter because he was thinking of her, too, and the love he had in his heart for her was the present and the future.

'Is that the yes I want to hear?'

'Yes,' she said with a commitment she carried to his lips.

It was a kiss that released all the tension of the evening and replaced it with a wondrous welling of emotion, flowing from one to the other with every touch, every breath, every beat of their hearts. The ultimate two-way street, Ashley thought, and knew she would give Harry however many children he wanted, because deep down in the roots of his being, his ancestry and the long-held heritage at Springfield Manor meant a lot to him.

Happy and confident that everything was settled to their mutual satisfaction, Ashley decided that Harry could do with a bit of chiding for his lengthy masquerade. 'And just when were you going to tell me the truth about yourself, Harold Alistair Cliffton?'

'On my home ground.' He grinned. 'I always play the advantage.'

'You thought Springfield Manor would sway me?'

'No. It simply kept the ball rolling my way until you were ready to acknowledge you didn't want a life without me.'

'Well, it should be interesting to meet George,' she mused.

'Why?'

'Because he started it all, didn't he? We wouldn't have met except for George. One could say it's a classic case of the butler did it.'

'I think it was I, pretending to be the butler, who did it,' Harry said, cocking one eyebrow in wicked humour.

Ashley laughed and wound her arms around his neck, swaying against him teasingly. 'Let's see if you can do it again.'

'What a splendid idea! I think I'll start with this little bow at your waist . . .'

'Wait!'

'You have some better idea?'

'No, but after the stands you and William took tonight, we should pull down the blinds.'

CHAPTER FOURTEEN

GEORGE Fotheringham was exceedingly pleased with himself. It had been his initiative that had inspired Master Harry to go off on such a fortuitous venture. Producing the Black Sheep with the Australian heir had, indeed, been a master card. Although one could not underestimate the drawing power of the accompanying photographs.

George had them on the table in front of him, trophies, one might say, of his astute judgement. Miss Ashley was a fine-looking woman—intelligence in her eyes, character in her face—and her feminine qualities were more than presentable. As a wife for Master Harry, George had no doubt she would do him credit. And the boy was proof that she was fertile. Such a relief to be sure of that. Poor Miss Pen... But thankfully that was in the past now.

Springfield Manor was going to be a happy place again. The whole staff had brightened up with the prospect of Master Harry bringing home a fiancée. And the boy. A child did liven up a home. George nodded approvingly at the photograph of William. He looked a bright young spark. George fancied he discerned a family likeness there, a certain set about the eyes. Amazing how genes could pop up generations down the line.

Mischief and mayhem.

George frowned. Now why had those words slid into his mind? Master Harry was about to embrace marriage and fatherhood, both of which had a sobering influence on any man. Unseemly antics were definitely at an end. Life at Springfield Manor was about to enter a new, productive cycle.

The telephone rang. George had been waiting for the call. He felt his heart lift in anticipation as he picked up the receiver. It was the expected message.

Cook and Mrs. Fotheringham were conferring in the kitchen, and several maids were standing by for further orders when George emerged from the private sanctum of the butler's pantry. He clapped his hands to gain the appropriate respectful attention, then made his announcement.

'Ten minutes, everyone. Spread the word. Ten minutes. And mind that you're all tidy.'

Ashley thought she was prepared for it. Twenty-six acres of gardens and parkland, Harry had told her. He didn't know how many rooms there were in Springfield Manor—George or his wife, the housekeeper, could undoubtedly tell her—but only part of it dated back to the thirteenth century. It had been added to by various ancestors. One of its features was a domed tower by Christopher Wren. The whole of the inside had been thoroughly modernised by Harry's parents, who had drowned in a ferry disaster in the North Sea.

The manor was set in a wooded valley of the Southern Cotswolds, and there was trout fishing in the river. A heated swimming pool and an all-weather tennis court provided other outdoor leisure activities. Inside, a well-stocked library, a billiards room and a solarium were places of interest to guests. William would like the minstrel gallery, where quite a few ghosts had appeared over the years.

George would be able to tell her how many staff were employed. It was George's responsibility to see to maintenance and the efficient running of the household. For all practical purposes, George ruled the manor, and he was excessively proud of it.

Ashley took a deep breath as the Rolls turned through a massive stone gateway. This was what Roger and his mother had wanted but didn't know how to achieve, coming back home to England. She wondered if they somehow knew that William, unbeknownst to him, was achieving their ambition, about to receive all the benefits that had been lost so many generations ago. Although Ashley would make sure it didn't go to his head!

The two-hour trip from London had flown by, and Springfield Manor now lay straight ahead of them. It was a mind-boggling sight, huge, like three or four mansions joined together. Apart from the domed tower, most of it was two storeys high, plus the attic area under the steep roofs from which rose a forest of chimneys. The spacious lawns leading up to it were as smooth as bowling greens, and behind it was woodland with immense, majestic trees that must have been growing since King Arthur was a boy.

In front of the manor a long line of people stretched out from what was clearly the main entrance. 'Uh-oh!' Harry sighed. 'George has decided this is an occasion. Consider yourself welcomed and honoured, Ashley. You're to be greeted by everyone on the staff. At least, all those who are readily available.'

'I count twenty-seven,' William said helpfully. He had always been good at numbers.

'What do I say to them?' Ashley asked, nervous at the prospect of meeting so many people at once, people who would be eyeing her in the context of future mistress of the manor.

Harry smiled at her. 'Don't worry. They're predisposed to think you're the best thing that could happen to them. George will lead you down the receiving line and make the introductions. Smile, say hello, repeat their names and answer any remark made with something friendly. You've probably done it thousands of times when meeting prospective clients. It isn't any different.'

His confidence boosted hers. All the same, she was very glad they had stopped over in London for a few days to shop for suitable clothes for the English winter, even more glad that Harry had insisted on buying them for her, steering her straight into designer outfits.

Her burgundy-coloured overcoat was elegantly tailored, and Ashley adored the matching suede boots and the perky hat with its smartly curved brim. For the hat to sit properly she had to wear her hair down, which Harry preferred anyway. She glanced at the dazzling diamond on the third finger of her left hand and decided to leave both gloves off. The fabulous engagement ring Harry had given her definitely reinforced her position as his future wife.

She gave her son a quick check before the Rolls came to a halt. William looked astonishingly smart in a double-breasted navy overcoat, white shirt and tie and long trousers. It was cold enough for him not to demur at wearing such unaccustomed clothes. Besides, Harry was similarly attired, and Harry could do no wrong in William's eyes. Not in the present propitious circumstances.

The chauffeur opened the door for Harry, who then helped Ashley out of the car. William followed under his own steam. A buzz of excitement ran down the greeting line at first sight of them.

A most impressive figure of a man stepped forward from the head of it. He was taller than Harry, broad-shouldered, barrel-chested, black-suited and enormously dignified. He looked to be in his fifties, although his benign face was relatively unwrinkled. Beneath the iron-grey eyebrows that matched his iron-grey hair, a pair of bright brown eyes bestowed approval.

'Welcome home, Master Harry,' he intoned, as though it was a highly portentous occasion.

Harry gripped his hand. 'Well done, George,' he replied with a tinge of amusement. 'May I present Ashley Harcourt, my fiancée, and her son, William. Our butler, George Fotheringham.'

'I'm delighted to meet you, George,' Ashley said, offering her best smile and her hand, which was quickly and warmly enveloped.

'Your coming is a pleasure that has been much looked forward to, Miss Ashley. We at Springfield Manor will do all we can to make you feel comfortable and at home.'

'That's very kind.'

'And your son, too, of course. How do you do, young William?'

'I'm fine, sir,' William replied, shaking hands without so much as batting an eyelash. Ashley was proud of his good manners until he piped up with, 'How many ghosts have you seen in the minstrel gallery, Mr. Fotheringham?'

'Not now, William,' she reproved.

The butler raised his eyebrows at Harry.

'Runs in the family, George,' he answered. 'It didn't die out on the other side of the world. No rest for you, I'm afraid.'

'What didn't die out?' Ashley asked, bewildered by the understanding the two men obviously shared.

George looked at her with rueful resignation. 'Mischief and mayhem, Miss Ashley. It has been the lot of the Fotheringhams down through the centuries, since the Battle of Flodden in 1513, to rescue Master Harry's family line from the mischief and mayhem they have invariably indulged in and brought upon themselves. If Henry Cliffton hadn't stirred up the Scottish pikemen with insults about what was under their kilts...' He sighed. 'So it has always been, Miss Ashley.'

'Look at it this way, George,' Harry blithely invited. 'It's another challenge for you. You'll be in good training by the time Ashley and I produce the patter of little feet.'

'Master Harry,' said George very dryly, 'I cannot recall ever being *out* of training.' He waved to the waiting line. 'Shall we proceed, sir?'

Ashley was introduced to George's wife, Alice, the head housekeeper, who organised and supervised all the cleaning, the meals and whatever services family and guests required. Then came innumerable maids, valets, footmen, the head gardener, the under-gardener and so on. Ashley committed as many names as she could to memory and hoped that the staff's obvious goodwill towards her would stretch into good-natured patience when she made mistakes.

In the next few hours, Ashley was introduced to the style of life at Springfield Manor. It was luxury to a standard she could not have imagined. Gordon Payne's appraisal of the private art collection was probably a modest one, and she had certainly been right about antiques. Everywhere she looked, they graced rooms and hallways alike.

The furnishings were nothing short of fabulous, satins and silks and velvets and brocades. There were huge marble fireplaces, oak panelling, painted ceilings, wonderful Persian carpets. She was dazed by a multitude of splendours.

A maid was assigned to take care of her personal needs. Her luggage was unpacked for her. Lancombe toiletries were provided in an ensuite bathroom that even contained a spa bath.

George presided over the serving of a gourmet lunch and an exquisite afternoon tea. The latter was lingered over in a wonderful sitting room in front of a huge log fire. Floor-to-ceiling windows looked out over a rose garden hedged by ornamental shrubs. Darkness gradually shrouded the view, the winter night falling quite early.

Ashley went up to her bedroom to have a rest and change before dinner. She stripped off her arrival clothes, enjoyed a long spa bath, then, leaving only a dim table lamp on, she stretched out on the luxurious four-poster bed to relax for a while and adjust herself to becoming used to the riches around her. It seemed incredible that this was going to be her life from now on.

She wondered if William could be dissuaded from staying up all night in the minstrel gallery. It was unlikely, with Harry and George aiding and abetting him and the whole staff adopting a light-hearted approach to the coming adventure.

A movement caught her eye. She turned her head in time to see a figure materialising through the heavily carved door that led into her bedroom. She blinked in sheer disbelief. But her eyes weren't playing tricks with her.

The insubstantial figure quickly took on more solid form, a woman, a young woman dressed in a long button-through skirt, blouse and cardigan, all of them oddly colourless. She was painfully thin yet her face, framed by short soft wavy hair, had an ethereal beauty, and her eyes seemed to glow as though lit by some otherworldly vision.

Slowly and warily, Ashley pushed herself into a sitting position, hardly daring to accept that a ghost had appeared in front of her. But what else could the woman be? And Harry had said there were ghosts at Springfield Manor.

The woman smiled at her. And spoke. 'I'm sorry if I gave you a fright. I should have knocked. But one gets so used to walking through walls and doors. Indeed, I wouldn't know how to tap on your door even if I wanted to.'

Ashley wished William was here to see this.

'Your William is in the kitchen,' the ghost said with a tinkling laugh. 'I've been down there listening to the gossip about you. I wish I could have been at Olivia Stanton's party. It must have been a wonderful scene.'

'William's telling them about that?'

'He kept Dylan Stanton's tooth and he produced it with the air of a master magician playing his ultimate trick.'

'Oh, no! He couldn't!'

'Don't worry. Everyone loved it. I think another legend has been born, with both William and Harry as the heroes.'

She could be right about that, Ashley thought. After all, it couldn't be much more outrageous than some of the other legends she'd heard about the family.

'Besides,' the ghost went on, 'they're dying to hear all about your romance with Harry, and William is earning favours with every tale he tells. There's no harm being done, believe me.'

Ashley released a shaky breath. She didn't know ghosts could read minds, too. It was disconcerting, to say the least. 'Who are you?' she asked.

'Penelope. Harry told you about me in great detail.'

'Yes. Yes, he did. I'm so sorry...'

'It wasn't to be,' she said sadly.

'Have you...' Ashley swallowed hard. 'Have you appeared to Harry?'

'No. That would have made things worse for him. I desperately wanted him to meet someone like you whom he could love as deeply as he's capable of loving.'

'You don't mind?'

'I'm happy for you both. Very happy. I've been waiting all this time for it to happen. It's a great relief to me now that it has.' Her smile was strangely luminous. 'And the baby makes it perfect.'

'What baby?'

'You're pregnant, Ashley. If you want to check it out, I can recommend a local medical practitioner, Dr. Jekyll. He lives in the village in Mr. Hyde's cottage. He was so good to me during my illness. He'll take every care with both of you.'

Ashley shook her head in bemusement. She let the Jekyll-Hyde connection float over her head. Nothing about Springfield Manor and its environs was going to surprise her any more. She honed in on the important point. If she was pregnant, it must have happened when she and Harry had first made love together.

Penelope nodded. 'Yes. I'll leave you now. I just wanted to meet you and satisfy my curiosity. And assure you there's nothing to fear from Harry's memories of me. They no longer have the power to hurt. Love has no boundaries. Love holds no restrictions, only those self-imposed by people. Harry loves you. Never doubt it, Ashley. He loves you.'

'You don't resent that I'm going to have all the happiness that was once rightfully yours?' Ashley asked.

Penelope's smile held no reservations. 'In my condition strange things happen. I will have that happiness in ways you cannot possibly understand.'

'You don't mind my being pregnant?'

'The bringing of life to Springfield Manor is the greatest joy of all.'

The sincerity in her voice convinced Ashley that this was rightly so. 'You're so unforgettably beautiful,' she couldn't help saying.

'So are you. Don't be alarmed. I can assure you through means that I cannot reveal that I will not interfere with your future happiness. In fact, in this part of the universe it works quite the opposite way. If you ever need help or someone to talk to, I'll come to you, Ashley. I want us to be friends.'

'Yes.' Ashley was not about to disagree with that.

'It's very simple really,' Pen explained. 'My love for Harry now joins yours.'

Ashley didn't see her dematerialise. She was there. Then she had passed through the solid oak door and was gone. Ashley wondered if she'd dreamt the visitation, but how could she have when she was sitting up in bed wide awake? She pinched herself to make sure. It hurt. Either she was having hallucinations or it had actually happened. Well, there was one way of finding out.

Ashley dressed as quickly as she could. She left her bedroom and went to Harry's. He was sliding his arms into a gorgeous teal blue jacket as she entered. He grinned at her, his eyes dancing wickedly. 'You beat me to a visit.'

She dithered. Should she let sleeping dogs lie?

The twinkle faded as he frowned. 'Is something wrong, Ashley?'

There could be no harm in it. Penelope had told her so. If ghosts could be believed. Besides, ghosts needed to be laid to rest, as well. 'Do you have a photograph of your Pen, Harry?'

'Yes.'

'May I see it?'

The frown deepened. 'Ashley...'

'Please?'

He shrugged off his concern. 'If you wish.' He went to a bureau drawer and drew out a framed photograph. 'This was taken towards the end. Pen was very thin by then.'

Ashley took one look and knew she hadn't hallucinated. 'Yes,' she said. 'That's her.' The same beautiful face and soft wavy hair. Even the same clothes, although they were coloured in the photograph.

'Mum! Mum! Where are you?' The call from William was loud, breathless and excited.

She quickly handed the photograph to Harry and hurried to the wide corridor that ran the length of this bedroom wing. 'I'm here, William.'

He came pelting out of her bedroom. 'Mum! Guess what? I saw a ghost. And I wasn't even hunting for one.'

'Where?' she asked sharply.

'Downstairs. I was having a look at all the old stuff in the great hall and I saw her zap straight through the doors into the sitting room.'

'Her? A woman with short, wavy hair?'

'Yes. But she was definitely a ghost, Mum. The doors were closed. I chased after her but when I went into the sitting room, no-one was there.'

'Are you sure?'

'No kidding, Mum. It was a ghost. I'm going to find Mr. Fotheringham. He might know who she is.'

He was off again just as Harry joined her outside his bedroom. 'What was that all about?'

'A ghost in the sitting room.' She flashed a look of entreaty at Harry. She wanted his belief. 'It was Pen, Harry. She's saying goodbye. She came to me about half an hour ago.'

He searched her eyes for several tense moments, then accepted her statement without equivocation. 'Let's go down to the sitting room. She liked lying on the chaise longue by the windows, watching the roses bloom and the daffodils in flower on the lawn. Nature's sunlight. She loved the sunlight. She always brought light wherever she was.'

That was where they found her, right at the far end of the room in a soft glow of light. She rose from the chaise longue and turned to them both, more ghostly than before.

'It's all right, Harry,' she softly soothed. 'I'm not here to haunt you. I never wanted to.'

'Why now, Pen? Why didn't you allow me to see you sooner?' he asked gruffly.

'I wanted you to let go, Harry. You had so much more of life to live. Your grief kept me here,' she said sadly, then slowly a smile grew, glowing with

the most incandescent benevolence. 'Your happiness...your love for Ashley and hers for
you...releases me from the chains of your grief.
My soul is now free to soar. I wish you and Ashley
every happiness in the world. Don't waste it. Never
waste it.'

She began to fade.

'Pen...' Harry reached out to her.

'It's loving that's life, Harry. Loving...' It was
barely a wisp of sound, a wisp that shimmered for
a moment, then disappeared.

The ensuing silence was fraught with swirling
emotions.

'Loving,' Harry murmured at last, and slowly
drew Ashley into his embrace. 'We must never let
anything get in the way of loving, Ashley.'

'No. We never will, Harry. Pen told me something else, too.'

'What?'

'She advised me to see Dr. Jekyll in the village.'

'There's nothing wrong, is there?' he asked
anxiously.

'No. Something very right. Pen said I was
pregnant, Harry. I'm only two days overdue. I can't
be certain. But Pen was quite definite that we'd
made a baby.'

He smiled. The smile grew into a grin, then a
chuckle, then a burst of happy laughter. 'I hope
you're pleased, my love, because I can't help feeling
I'm the luckiest man on earth.'

'And I'm the luckiest woman,' Ashley said fervently.

A long way away, their kiss was sensed, a pure bonding of souls, an explosion of joy and love, and the being who had been known as Penelope was content.

The thought came to Ashley that for all the years she and Harry lived at Springfield Manor, a vase of roses or daffodils would be placed beside the chaise longue in the sitting room.

There was a knock on the door. William rushed in, followed more sedately by George. 'Any ghosts in here, Master Harry?' George inquired.

'Not at the moment, George.' He smiled at William. 'It will have to be the minstrel gallery tonight. Eric the Red might pay us a visit if we're lucky.'

'Indeed, yes.' George tactfully gathered William under his wing. 'Come. I shall show you the fireplace where Eric the Red split the mantel with his axe. Quite an exciting ghost, Eric.'

'Before you leave us, George . . .'

'Yes, Master Harry?'

'The bottle of 1860 Madeira we discussed before my trip to Australia. I think you've earned it, George.'

'How gracious of you, Master Harry!'

'And tell your good wife that a June wedding date is out. We'll be having the wedding much sooner. As soon as it can be suitably arranged, in fact.'

'I shall certainly drink to that, Master Harry.'

A self-satisfied smile played on George's lips as he ushered William out of the sitting room to give the happy couple some private time together. A duty well done, he thought.

Then, with intense pride, he added ... And, of course, the butler did it.

The *Times*
Personal Column
Births

Cliffton—On 14 October to Ashley and Harold, a fine son, Edward John, at 8:10 p.m., and a beautiful daughter, Emily Louise, at 8:20 p.m. A brother and sister for William.

Coming Next Month

HARLEQUIN PRESENTS®

#1821 UNWANTED WEDDING Penny Jordan
(Top Author)
Rosy had to be married within three months. Guard Jamieson was successful, sexy—and single. With no other candidate available to walk her down the aisle, it looked as if Rosy would have to accept Guard's offer to help her out.

#1822 DEADLY RIVALS Charlotte Lamb
(Book Two: SINS)
When Olivia first met Max she was utterly captivated. But Max was her father's business enemy and she was forbidden to see him again. Four years later she agreed to marry Christos, Max's nephew. Then Max returned to claim her....

#1823 TWO'S COMPANY Carole Mortimer
(9 TO 5)
Juliet's boss has left her half his company but she has to share it with Liam, his son, who is sure that she seduced his father. Nor does she want him to know that she was engaged to his despised younger brother. Will he find out her dark secret?

#1824 A SAVAGE BETRAYAL Lynne Graham
(This Time, Forever)
Mina and Cesare had met again, four years after he rejected her as a gold-digging tramp! Now he was determined to marry her, but only to pursue his revenge on Mina.

#1825 SPRING BRIDE Sandra Marton
(Landon's Legacy: Book 4)
Kyra's father's legacy would allow her to assert her independence. Antonio would help her—but at a price! He wanted to own her completely—and if she succumbed Kyra knew she would never be free again.

#1826 PERFECT CHANCE Amanda Carpenter
(Independence Day)
Mary's life was reasonably happy—until the day Chance Armstrong walked into it! He was offering her the perfect chance for a lot of excitement and the most exciting challenge of all.... He asked Mary to marry him!

Mina and Cesare Falcone had met again, four
years after he had rejected her as a gold digger

BUT

He's back!

This time it'll be different

This time it'll be forever!

#1824 A Savage Betrayal
by Lynne Graham

Available in July wherever

HARLEQUIN ⬥ PRESENTS®

books are sold

If you are looking for more titles by

EMMA DARCY

Don't miss these fabulous stories by one of
Harlequin's most renowned authors:

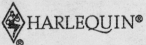